THE DEATH SPANCEL

The Death Spancel
and Others
by

Katharine Tynan

Swan River Press
Dublin, Ireland
MMXXI

The Death Spancel
by Katharine Tynan

Published by
Swan River Press
Dublin, Ireland
in October MMXXI

www.swanriverpress.ie
brian@swanriverpress.ie

Introduction © Peter Bell, MMXX
This edition © Swan River Press, MMXX

Dust jacket design by Meggan Kehrli
from artwork by Brian Coldrick

Set in Garamond by Ken Mackenzie

Published with assistance from Dublin UNESCO
City of Literature and Dublin City Libraries

ISBN 978-1-78380-754-3

Swan River Press published
a limited hardback of
The Death Spancel in November 2020.

Contents

Introduction	vii
Peter Bell	
The First Wife	3
The Dead Mother	9
The Sea's Dead	12
The Dead Tryst	17
The Death Spancel	19
The Death-Watch	26
The Ghosts	27
A Bride from the Dead	33
Miss Mary	45
The Ghost	55
A Sentence of Death	57
The Dead Coach	68
The Body Snatching	70
The Ghost	82
The Spancel of Death	98
The Dream House	114
The Call	127
A Night in the Cathedral	128
The Little Ghost	140
The Little Ghost	156
The Picture on the Wall	158
The Fields of My Childhood . . .	173

Sweet Singer from Over the Sea	181
Ghost Story of a Novelist	185
Dunsany	187

❦

Sources	197
Acknowledgements	201
About the Author	203

Introduction

Katharine Tynan (1859-1931) was one of Ireland's most prolific authors, writing almost a hundred novels, five volumes of autobiography, numerous poems, and hundreds of short stories and articles for a variety of journals, newspapers, and magazines. Whilst highly respected, her work cannot be said to have attained the status of classic literature, and little of it is still read today. Like many an author, she wrote because of a compulsive love of the craft; poetry at first, thereafter finding expression mainly in novels, books for girls, and the kind of short stories in demand for the era's most fashionable medium: popular fiction magazines. While this market may have tailored her fiction, it also provided a source of income—most welcome after being widowed with three children in January 1919. Tynan can be seen in the same category as several other authors of the late-nineteenth and early-twentieth centuries, including Mary Elizabeth Braddon and Edith Nesbit, or Irish writers such as Charlotte Riddell and L. T. Meade. The genres they wrote in produced general fiction, covering various popular themes: romance, intrigue, inheritance, family feuds, curses, legend, mystery, and the supernatural.

Supernatural literature in Ireland at the turn of the century was inextricably woven with a host of other themes: love, death, tragedy, remorse, vengeance, penance, and religious faith. Thus it forms a central presence, sometimes overtly, often subtly, in the output of such authors. A revived interest over recent decades in lost or forgotten supernatural fiction, as well as growing respect for the female practitioners of such tales, has led publishers, especially the small presses, to reprint them in definitive collections. Notable is Sarob Press's "Mistresses of the Macabre" series; two volumes by Irish writers, B. M. Croker and Rosa Mulholland, both of which were reissued by Swan River Press. Researched and anthologised by the late Richard Dalby, ghost story expert *par excellence*, they are the product of decades of hunting through numerous periodicals. Another writer logically destined for the series, whom Richard, shortly before he died in 2017, hoped would be collected, was Katharine Tynan.

The reasons why Richard did not get round to putting such an anthology together, and indeed for Tynan's neglect by a generation of anthologists of uncanny tales, are twofold. Firstly, Tynan's stories appeared in a wide variety of ephemeral magazines, some vanishingly scarce, making research a daunting task. Being meticulous, keen to be comprehensive, Richard did not find time to address such a project to his satisfaction. Tynan wrote over a dozen collections, most exceedingly difficult to find. Of her earliest volumes, only *An Isle in the Water* (1895) seems readily accessible; *Land of Mist and Mountain* (1895) and *Led by a Dream* (1899) are rare to the point of extinction. Tynan, moreover, is conspicuous by her absence in the many classic supernatural anthologies of the past century, an exception being "The Picture in the House" (1895) included in Montague Summers' *Victorian Ghost Stories* (1933); nor do her stories feature much in Irish fiction anthologies. All her novels are out of print, many unobtainable; nor was her work championed by Virago Press in its pioneering series of forgotten female authors.

Secondly, Tynan was by no means committed to the supernatural genre *per se*. She compiled no collection dedicated to her supernatural tales, as did other writers of the time.

Introduction

Indeed, only a fraction of her stories fall, even on a wide definition, into this category. In her short story collections, where content does address the supernatural, it is subsumed within what she called "sketches of Irish life", which include its legends and superstitions.

The ghostly, macabre, and uncanny, however, do feature in a significant portion of her writing. E. F. Bleiler, in his *Checklist of Science-Fiction and Supernatural Fiction*, lists only *An Isle in the Water* (1895), and a novel about ghostly possession, *The Heiress of Wyke* (1926). *The Moated Grange* (1925), reprinted in a Collins pocket edition in 1932 as *The Night of Terror*, is another foray into the supernatural; its new title inviting such expectation. A young Irish woman and her mother move into a lonely Suffolk mansion, Moated Grange, run by a sinister caretaker and his wife, seeming to be guarding a dark secret. The girl, who appears psychic, witnesses several deftly sketched apparitions, eerie rather than malevolent: a woman on the lakeside, and a wraith leaning over her mother as she plays the piano; there are also sinister rooms, never used, associated with a previous lady of the house; and a mysterious windmill, its great sails moving at night, hones this eeriness. The plot, however, is less concerned with the ghosts than the practical skulduggery of the caretaker and the mysterious neurosis of his wife, concerning her husband's malignity and a deceased child. Tynan skilfully invests both house and landscape with an ominous atmosphere, and the apparitions are subtly limned. Passages of terror are convincing, and she successfully conveys ambiguity and mystery, adroitly sketching the uncanny atmosphere of a house with a tragic history.

Although few of her novels directly address the supernatural, several deal with the mysterious, the uncanny, and the sinister. Strange old houses that might just be haunted form a frequent setting: like *The Curse of Castle Eagle* (1915),

Castle Perilous (1928), *The House in the Forest* (1928), and *The House of Dreams* (1934). Tynan displays an astute sense of place, elegantly finessing the *genius loci*, whether of the Irish countryside, or fog-bound London. Supernatural events, prophecies, curses, apparitions, as well as a general sense of the weird and ghastly occur even in her "realistic" stories, suggesting the imagination and stylistic flare of a "Mistress of the Macabre". Her novels for girls likewise occasionally show a sinister touch. In *Bitha's Wonderful Year* (1921), a young girl encounters in London "a black fog" which she finds "peculiarly terrifying". This sustained prose passage—as, beset by panic, her senses eerily heightened, "surrounded by the strange shadow-shapes that emerged from the fog only to be engulfed again"; she becomes aware of "something shambling beside her", and "could not have told whether the thing was man or beast"—is a masterpiece of brooding terror, and as potent a description of a London fog as Charles Dickens's own at the beginning of *Bleak House* (1852/3) or Margery Allingham's in *The Tiger in the Smoke* (1952).

Katharine Tynan was born on 23 January 1859 in South Dublin. Her father, Andrew, was a livestock farmer, who doted on his daughter, one of eleven children; while her mother, Elizabeth, was "a large, placid, fair woman, who became an invalid at an early age and influenced my life scarcely at all" (*Twenty-Five Years*).

Tynan wrote five volumes of autobiography, offering a perceptive view of a crucial period of Irish history, straddling the 1916 Easter Rising; but most relevant to the present book is a profusion of insights into the Dublin literary scene and cultural *zeitgeist* of the late-nineteenth century, which profoundly influenced this budding young writer. Lord Dunsany, William Sharp, Oscar Wilde, Sarah Purser, Rosa Mulholland, George William Russell (A.E.), J. B. and W. B. Yeats, and other iconic names are there; as are the

Dublin Theosophists, like Rose Kavanagh, meeting at the weekly *soir*ées of John and Ellen O'Leary. This heady mix of mystical, occult, and literary intellect provided the seed-bed in which Tynan thrived. It is the first volume, *Twenty-Five Years* (1913), published at the age of fifty-two, covering her youth up to 1890, that offers most useful insight into those defining ideas and influences, and where can be discerned, amid her wealth of anecdote and reflection, matters and experiences that explain her fascination with the uncanny.

"Out of the dim mists and shadows of early childhood," she wrote, "there stand out clearly certain memories". One of her earliest recollections, a numinous experience, as it were, was of a blood-red aurora, and being "carried out wrapped up in shawls to see the great flames shooting up the sky". The fascination with eerie old houses, apparent in her books, possibly dates back to her first school, which was in "one of those toppling Dublin houses". A former country residence engulfed by the city, it "stood up, dark and dreaming, at the end of the garden, which had long lost its garden-beds and possessed only a few stunted lilacs and a sycamore".

When Tynan was eight years old, her father acquired "Whitehall", a comfortable country estate in Clondalkin, on the outskirts of Dublin, which immediately beguiled her. Here originated her mystic empathy with wild places, and that acute sense of *genius loci*, often fearful, recurrent in her writing. Especially disquieting was the moat where she went blackberrying:

> "Gathering them one never liked to be far from one's companions, lest harm befell. In the evening when it was dark it was pleasant to steal out and see the darkness of the Moat at a distance: and when the misted harvest moon rose above it we thought it was a fairy fire and it afforded a marvel for days to come."

This defining time and place she had previously eulogised in "The Fields of My Childhood", an atmospheric piece that concludes *An Isle in the Water*. There was "an old fort on a little hill, a noted resort of the fairies", where in the summer gloaming "you might see their hundreds of little lamps threading a fantastic measure in and out on the rath . . . which floated away if any were bold enough to approach them, like glorified balls of that thistledown of which children divine what's o'clock". The moat possessed,

> "an uncanniness of its own, haunted by leaping fires that overran it and left no trace. You might see it from afar, suffused by a dull glare, any dim summer night. So have I myself beheld it when I have crept through the dews on a nocturnal expedition."

It can be speculated this influential memory inspired the setting for her macabre novel, *The Moated Grange*. The fascination with fairy lore, of course, was deeply rooted in Irish tradition, an interest she shared with many of the Dublin *literati*, including her lifelong friend, W. B. Yeats (1865-1939).

Tynan's concern with the supernatural, particularly of the more baleful kind, dated back to her childhood: "I was brought up on the dreadful churchyard stories of the Irish peasant imagination." Elsewhere she wrote how she and her siblings used to "creep up the dark stairs to bed in a shivering string, each child trying to be in the middle and not first or last". She was taken to wakes, expected to kiss the deceased: "I saw more dead people in my childhood than I ever saw in youth or maturity." It, she dryly observed, "did not tend to a freedom from nerves". A "gruesome experience" was being taken to see the hangman's drop at Dublin Gaol; as well as a "peculiarly dreadful hospital, for the sick people were mainly suffering from delirium tremens", that "coloured unpleasantly some of my childhood dreams". Her grandparents believed in ghosts, and her father, a compelling raconteur, told ghostly tales with "a curious impressiveness", of Cheeverstown, "which had its rath, its ghosts and fairies", and a strange ancient tower amid "dream-haunted fields". Years later, in her twenties, she reluctantly attended a séance, where malevolent spirits objected to her presence; it was a disturbing experience: "I was quite determined to be in opposition to the whole thing, to disbelieve in it, and disapprove of it as playing with things of life and death," yet she witnessed apparently authentic phenomena. Glad to escape, the last thing she noticed was Willie Yeats "banging his head on the table as though he had a fit, muttering to himself". How far Tynan believed in spirits is uncertain, though she was a devoted Roman Catholic, in awe of Christianity's mystical aspects. She appears to have kept an open mind, but like her father (who was sceptical), maintained a certain fascination with the supernatural evident in her tales, which sometimes exhibit a touch of the grisly.

Tynan was growing up and writing at a critical time in Irish history, when politics and religion were fusing in the violent struggles of nationalism. A firm Catholic, she nevertheless had good Protestant friends, and was of a tolerant liberal persuasion. While sympathetic to the nationalist cause, she shrank from its extreme forms, and deplored violence. An early memory was overhearing talk about riots in Belfast, when "women's ear-rings were pulled through the lobes of their ears". But there is a passage in the story "A Prodigal Son", collected in *An Isle in the Water*, expressing outrage at Protestant-driven emigration:

> "They are always, with their mistaken philanthropy, drafting away the boys and girls from Ireland, to cast them, human wreckage, in the streets of New York; always taking away the young life from the sweet glens

over which the chapel bell sends its shepherding voice, and casting it away in noisome places, while at home the aged folk go down alone to the grave."

Although she was politically aware, and her later memoirs contain shrewd cameos of political figures, as well as a good deal of perceptive history, her novels and stories generally avoid overt political matters; in contrast to another Irish supernatural author, Dorothy Macardle (1889-1958), whose spectral tales reflect her ardent nationalism.

Tynan's passion for the mystique of Roman Catholicism was intricately associated with the death of her eldest sister, Mary, her "first love", while home from her convent school. "Something of the innocency and fragrance of the convent," she wrote, "hung about her, making her elusive, saint-like." Mary was "a brief lovely vision", who "let me see just a glimpse of her supernatural secret". There was "something heavenly in the vision, something of long convent corridors, dazzlingly clean, flooded with light and air, sweet with the smell of lilies and a thought of incense, of little convent cells naked and pure, of convent gardens, places where 'The Brides of Christ / Lie hid, emparadised'." It was "my first intimate experience with death". "Desolation swept my soul for a space. I do not know how long." At the age of twelve, she began convent school herself in Drogheda. Its crucial formative impact on her is testified to by the many pages she devotes to her experience there, which lasted until she was fourteen.

Tynan's abiding memory was one of "heavenly ecstasy":

"The convent school remains in my mind as a place of large and lofty rooms, snow-white, spotless, full of garden airs: of long corridors lit by deep windows, with little altars here and there—statues of Our Lord or the Blessed Virgin or the Saints, each with flowers. A blue lamp burned at Our Lady's feet. The Sacred Heart had its twinkling red lamp. The corridors seem always in my thoughts of them full of quietness. The rustling of the nun's habit as she came only added to the quietness."

The cloister was segregated from the school by curtained entries that filled her with a certain awe: "Through the veils of the door you could see the shadowy figures of the nuns moving along the corridor beyond." Iris Murdoch's novel, *The Bell* (1958), set in such an establishment, contains a similarly eerie scene, in which presences move mysteriously behind a separating screen.

These eerie impressions were complemented by others, more macabre. Peeping one night from a high dormitory window, she perceived over the wall of the nuns' cemetery the marble slab listing the names of deceased nuns: "Of winter nights it used to glimmer whitely in the dark." There was always about the memory "a chill feeling". The convent possessed two relics, one decidedly grisly upon which she feared to gaze: the head of Oliver Plunkett, Catholic Archbishop of Armagh, a martyr of Titus Oates' conspiracy, his skull rescued from the fire by a loyal supporter. The other was of Saint Edward the Confessor, a linen cloth of alleged curative potency, with regard to which Tynan attributes a miracle, the healing of a youth from scrofula: "you may explain the happening as you will". A old nun, Sister Catherine, was mad, and of grotesque mien: "a fearsome apparition, for she went about bent almost double, her habit and veil, green with age, huddled upon her, as she leant on her stick, so that you caught a bare glimpse of a yellowed ivory face". There was an ancient organ, depicting Pan:

"Some good nun had clad the goat-footed god in a scarlet mantle, had placed a crown of gold upon his head, had changed the Pan-pipes to a harp. She had dressed him in the garments of King David; but oh! She had not changed his eyes or his expression. From his dark corner the goat-foot laughed at these innocencies."

Such passages illustrate not only Tynan's eye for the weird detail, but her talent for painting in atmospheric prose, shades of the uncanny.

Despite her life-long affliction of poor eyesight, Tynan was captivated by reading from an early age, initiated by her father's eloquent anecdotes. Yet her mother, reflecting a cultural prejudice of the time that saw reading as unfitting for women, positively discouraged her daughter, even securing the imprimatur of a doctor, who warned Katharine, if she kept on reading, of a dreadful consequence: "I should probably end up an idiot." This antipathy served only to fuel her voracious literary appetite. Her father "brought books into the house, miscellaneous lots picked up at auctions, of the most varied kind". As he rejected censorship, "I cannot recall that he ever told me not to read any book, although I must have read some curious ones under his eyes". His attitude was always "Let her be", while her mother's was "Don't". She recalled her mother locking away a romance she was enjoying, leaving "an impression which lasts to this day of a golden-haired lady in whose fortunes I had so passionate an interest that it was a cruel fate indeed to have my following of them cut short". Penny story papers, like *The London Reader*, *The London Journal*, *The Family Herald*, she smuggled into the house beneath her mother's "unsuspecting gaze", hiding them "pushed up between my frock and my stays," retreating to a loft over the stables, where she read them in "dusty darkness with the most delightful sense of freedom".

The family library comprised many books, which she devoured, even dry political material as well as classics,

Introduction

confessing that she preferred William Meinhold's gothic novel *Sidonia the Sorceress* (1847; which Lady Wilde translated in 1849) to Jane Austen. Befriending two ladies who kept a shop that stocked, in addition to groceries, books and magazines, and which hosted a circulating library, Tynan was seduced: "Even now I can feel the ecstasy of touching those green and scarlet and blue backs of books and knowing that I might read what I would." In her late teens she discovered "a treasure of a library" at the Dublin Mechanic's Institute, where she read *Cornhill*, *Frazer's*, *St. Paul's*, "dear, delightful *Temple Bar*", as well as *Belgravia*, "with all the tales of Miss Braddon running through it". The librarian let her "roam the shelves at will and take away all I could carry", and her arm "sometimes shook for days after my book-getting expeditions because of the weight". Later, she discovered the Royal Dublin Society's library at Leinster House, with its "high, twisting, narrow corridor, lined to the dim richness of the ceiling with books", brought by a deferential librarian after whispered requests. Friendship with the literary family of author, Hannah French, brought Tynan her "first real touch with literature". Here she was introduced to the *Anatomy of Melancholy* (1621) and the *Religio Medici* (1642). Tynan, at school, "sucked dry" whatever "honey was to be got out of the convent library", much of which was dull fare, yet from *Lives of the Saints* she "carried away a store of beautiful legends". Thus, from this diverse cornucopia of reading, Tynan acquired the eclecticism that hallmarks her diverse literary output.

Tynan ascribes the beginning of her literary career to the Jesuit, Father Matthew Russell (1834-1912), to whom she sent a poem based on her convent learning, concerning the Dominican, Blessed James of Ulm, which the priest published in the *Irish Monthly*. Russell introduced her to important literary contacts, notably his kinswoman, Rosa Mulholland (1841-1921), who became a lifetime friend and mentor to Katharine. Mulholland, a frequent contributor to Dickens's *All the Year Round*, had written highly regarded ghost stories, and it is likely these too influenced Tynan's forays in the genre. "I could scarcely believe in my own good fortune," she recalled, "when I was admitted to Miss Mulholland's friendship". Her acquaintance with someone who had "touched with high gods and goddesses", was so "dazzling to me that I could scarcely bear the light which flowed upon me". Mulholland introduced her to her best friend, the historian Sarah Atkinson (1823-1893), who inhabited a house fascinating Tynan, "built upon a sort of causeway ascended by many steps from the sunken roadway", creating the impression of "a house built high in the air". There were "books everywhere, in the hall, around the rooms, in niches on the staircase", a place where "one found the bookish atmosphere at its best, rarefied and sweetened by lofty spiritual faith and ideals". At this time Tynan saw herself as a poet, and Mulholland was an early voice prevailing upon her to try her hand at prose. She lacked the confidence until 1887, when Alfred Williams of the *Providence Journal*, an English émigré living in America, the author of a book on Celtic folklore, asked Katharine to write something for the periodical, where she discovered "the stars in the English literary sky while they were yet only on the horizon".

Tynan's first book was a volume of poetry, *Louise de la Vallière* (1885), which won her the admiration of leading figures in the Irish Revival, and was followed by numerous successful subsequent collections. It was, again, her father who introduced her to poetry, mostly of Irish nationalism; but her first poetic muses were Elizabeth Browning, Tennyson, Shelley, and (to the scorn of Yeats) Longfellow. In the Leinster House library, Tynan "read all the modern poetry I could lay my hands upon", including Swinburne, Morris, and Christina Rossetti; but after buying Swinburne's *Tristram of Lyonesse*

Introduction

(1882), she quickly disposed of it, finding it "a burden to my conscience". Christina Rossetti wrote her a fulsome letter praising *Louise de la Vallière*:

> "I can express my sincere admiration for your poetic gift. But beyond all gifts I account *graces*, and therefore the piety of your work fills me with hopes far beyond any to be raised by music or diction. If you have honoured my form by thinking it worth imitating, much more may I your spirit."

Tynan recalls going with one of her first royalty cheques, to some family disdain, straight to Hodges & Figgis, the Grafton Street booksellers, purchasing a volume of Rossetti's poems, which she carried home, "hugging it to my breast like a baby". Tynan's contemporary influences included W. B. Yeats, whom she described in *Twenty-Five Years* as "beautiful to look at with his dark face, its touch of vivid colouring, the night-black hair, the eager dark eyes"; and George William Russell (A.E.), whose mystic sensibility she shared, and who would later write a foreword to her *Collected Poems* (1930). She recalls that, when staying at Yeats's home, she used to be awakened at night by "a steady, monotonous sound rising and falling. It was Willie chanting poetry to himself in the watches of the night". The present volume includes a selection of her poems that resonate with the mystical and supernatural; themes similarly present in her ghost stories.

The stories included herein are drawn from a variety of magazines; several of which were collected in *An Isle in the Water* (1895)—"The First Wife", "The Sea's Dead", "The Death Spancel", and "The Fields of My Childhood". *An Isle*

in the Water presents a series of tales from Achill Island in the west of Ireland, possibly inspired by real anecdotes she had heard. They reflect a way of life, already passing in Tynan's youth, in which supernatural belief and superstition were an integral part. The finest story, "The Sea's Dead", is rather different from the following selections, an evocative eulogy to the ominous presence of the sea and its associated legends. It is an excellent tale, and one wishes she had written more about the superstitions of old Ireland.

One of Tynan's talents is her ability to mould the conventions of the traditional ghost story in an original way. "The First Wife" takes a familiar supernatural theme: a new bride uneasily aware of the lingering shadow in the household of a previous wife. It is, indeed, a motif of Daphne du Maurier's *Rebecca* (1938). What makes this ghost story successful is Tynan's subtle grasp of atmosphere; constructing an eerie presence without overt description of the phantom, manifest through impressions, sounds, and sensations, which the new wife struggles to deny. The ghost that remains unseen, as in Oliver Onions' "The Beckoning Fair One" (1911), is always more frightening than the graphic spectre. One of the oldest clichés in supernatural fiction is the supposed super-sensitivity of dogs to haunting; yet here, Tynan exploits the motif to poignant effect.

"A Sentence of Death" (1908), a tale of premonition, presents an oft-repeated plot in supernatural fiction. A sinister horse-drawn carriage arrives at night, its driver announcing "Room for one, Madame!" Tynan skilfully reflects the mental state of the young woman who experiences the apparition; it has a nice twist at the end. The same plot was used by E. F. Benson in his story "The Bus-Conductor" (1906). Tynan's ghost stories are notable for the way they mould ostensibly foreseeable plots in unexpected directions. "The Ghost" (1902), a seemingly simple love-match story, moves in an unpredictable, original manner, a complex tale in which music features as a mode of supernatural rescue. "The Little Ghost" (1913) utilises a sentimental motif of Victorian fiction, the ghost-child, but brings originality to the "alas, poor ghost" theme; a complex, poignant story with a psychological dimension, finessed by Tynan's command of style, imagery, and atmosphere. "The Dream House" (1909) is also cleverly plotted, inverting expectations: a woman dreams in astonishing detail of the inside of a house she has never seen—it comes on the market for a strange reason. "Miss Mary" (1903) is a melancholy tale of a young woman considered to have "something strange" about her, perhaps "so near the borders of a twilight world that it took but little shock to push her over altogether". The setting, partly in one of Tynan's favoured old estates, partly on the wild coast, redolent with fatal tragedies, strongly powers the story. "The Ghosts", which is an extract from Tynan's novel *The Story of Bawn* (1906), is not really a story, but a brief presentation of hauntings in the manner of a compilation of "true" tales, which is probably what they are. Of interest is one, in which the ghostly motif closely echoes in its phrasing a passage in "The First Wife": "the swish, swish of a silken gown on the stairs"—and in the "The Ghosts", "the swish of the satin as it went by my door".

Although Tynan makes only limited reference in her memoirs to writers who inspired her, her profuse and eclectic early reading undoubtedly included the gothic legacy, with such as Mrs. Radcliffe, Edgar Allan Poe, the Brontës, and Dublin's invisible prince, Joseph Sheridan Le Fanu (1814-1873); their voices resonate in many of her stories, which are often touched with the macabre, the grotesque, and the morbid, even when set within the context of the sentimental. The motif of body-snatching, when unscrupulous medical research created this grisly market, features in two tales: "The Body Snatching" (1902) and "A Bride from the Dead" (1910). In both cases an apparently deceased young woman is rescued from entombment as an indirect result of the practice, being in fact in a cataleptic stupor, a frequent theme of Poe. They are more in the vein of *Grand Guignol* than the supernatural. The former is set against the backdrop of smallpox-riven Dublin, skilfully sketched in two short paragraphs. The latter is a more complex and successful tale, moving deceptively through motifs of the ghost story, its plot twisting neatly to become a tale of the grotesque, raising alarming moral questions. The morbidity and beauty present in her description of the "corpse", reflects Tynan's intimate childhood encounters with death, especially that of her beloved sister, the dead whom one wishes could return to life.

Two selections with a gothic feel have almost the same title. But "The Death Spancel" (1895) and "The Spancel of Death" (1890), have different plots, using this grim artefact of Irish occult lore, a strip of skin from head to heel taken from a corpse to bind a prospective lover. In the former the sinner refuses to repent; in the latter there is death-bed absolution by the priest; both are infused with Roman Catholic mores, the Church triumphant over evil. They are effective because of Tynan's command of atmosphere. In "The Death Spancel", language and imagery are applied to great impact, producing sustained passages of macabre prose-poetry, most notable in the opening paragraphs; somewhat in the mode of Lady Dilke's gothic pieces in *The Shrine of Death* (1886). "The Picture on the Wall" (1895) centres round the common motif of a sinister portrait with eyes that pursue the observer, inducing ghastly nightmares; underlying the tale is a theme typical of this kind of terror tale, the shadow of inherited insanity. "A Night in the Cathedral" (1910) is pure horror, in which Tynan shows her capacity to create a sustained accumulation of horror; rather modern in its theme. With references to the Dean's "great predecessor who wrote the *Travels*" (Jonathan Swift) and the "miserable slum" only a stone's-throw away

Introduction

(the Liberties), the setting is clearly Saint Patrick's Cathedral in Dublin, "noble" and "Gothic", which for a time stood as a near ruin, "curious, damp, mouldering", until it was restored by the Guinness family in the 1860s. Finally, "The Fields of My Childhood", an elegiac memoir from *An Isle in the Water*, recalls her family's country house in Clondalkin, its *genius loci*, and is touched with beauty, awe, and mystery.

Three other pieces are included by way of appendices, which add to the ambience in which we may address Tynan's supernatural fiction. "Sweet Singers from Over the Sea" (1893) prints an interview with Tynan, containing literary insights; "Ghost Story of a Novelist" (1905) relates a weird tale at Trinity College Dublin experienced by one "near and dear" to Tynan; and "Dunsany", taken from her autobiography *The Year of the Shadow* (1919), offers insight into this guru of Irish fantasy fiction, as well as brief sketches of H. G. Wells and Sidney Sime.

Katharine Tynan married Henry ("Harry") Albert Hinkson, a barrister of the Inner Temple, in May 1893. The couple moved to England where they lived for the next eighteen years. They first settled in a blossom-shaded cottage in Ealing, with a "little gate" and a "huge St. Bernard" named "Paddy". Already an established writer, Tynan continued to support the family by her pen. Katharine and Henry bore five children, only three of whom lived; their daughter Pamela Hinkson (1900-1982) was also a successful novelist.

The family was once again living in Ireland when tragedy befell them in January 1919 and Henry died. Marilyn Rose Gaddis, an early biographer and critic, notes that Tynan writes about her husband with extreme reticence in her fourth autobiography, *The Wandering Years* (1922); "we deduce [his death] solely because she stops referring to him. The cause of death, the funeral, her grief are all too private to bear relating" (*Katharine Tynan*, 1974). After a long, distinguished career—and a short illness—Katharine Tynan died on 2 April 1931. She is buried in Saint Mary's Catholic Cemetery in Kensal Green, London.

☙

The Death Spancel and Others does not aspire to be definitive; given Tynan's vast output there may well be yet undiscovered stories. But it does offer a substantial representation of her weird tales. Although the supernatural forms only a small part of her writing, this collection is of great value for a full understanding of Tynan's literary legacy. Firstly, she is eclectic: these stories range across many themes categorised as supernatural: ghosts and hauntings; horror and the grotesque; legend and superstition; and various aspects of the uncanny. Secondly, while operating within recognisable formulae, she displays the imaginative capacity to step away from the predictable, and to eschew cliché; each story holds the attention, leading to an often surprising denouement. Thirdly, her command of prose is articulate and inventive; her writing often rings with a poetic timbre, bringing her narratives to life, infusing them with vivid imagery. They are, moreover, imbued with the power of the oral anecdote, which is how the eerie yarns of her homeland first engaged her imagination; her stories gain by being read aloud, finessing her compelling talent as a raconteur. This volume significantly increases our awareness of a much neglected and important literary figure of Ireland, and is a valuable addition to the portfolio of Irish supernatural authors published by Swan River Press.

Peter Bell
York, England
October 2020

The Death Spancel

The First Wife

The dead woman had lain six years in her grave, and the new wife had reigned five of them in her stead. Her triumph over her dead rival was well-nigh complete. She had nearly ousted her memory from her husband's heart. She had given him an heir for his name and estate, and, lest the bonny boy should fail, there was a little brother creeping on the nursery floor, and another child stirring beneath her heart. The twisted yew before the door, which was heavily buttressed because the legend ran that when it died the family should die out with it, had taken another lease of life, and sent out one spring green shoots on boughs long barren. The old servants had well-nigh forgotten the pale mistress who reigned one short year; and in the fishing village the lavish benefactions of the reigning lady had quite extinguished the memory of the tender voice and gentle words of the woman whose place she filled. A new era of prosperity had come to the Island and the race that long had ruled it.

Under a high, stately window of the ruined Abbey was the dead wife's grave. In the year of his bereavement, before the beautiful brilliant cousin of his dead Alison came and seized on his life, the widower had spent days and nights of stony despair standing by her grave. She had died to give him an heir to his name, and her sacrifice had been vain, for the boy came into the world dead, and lay on her breast in the coffin. Now for years he had not visited the place: the last wreaths of his mourning for her had been washed into earth and

The Death Spancel

dust long ago, and the grave was neglected. The fisherwives whispered that a despairing widower is soonest comforted; and in that haunted Island of ghosts and omens there were those who said that they had met the dead woman gliding at night along the quay under the Abbey walls, with the shape of a child gathered within her shadowy arms. People avoided the quay at night, therefore, and no tale of the ghost ever came to the ears of Alison's husband.

His new wife held him indeed in close keeping. In the first days of his re-marriage the servants in the house had whispered that there had been ill blood over the man between the two women, so strenuously did the second wife labour to uproot any trace of the first. The cradle that had been prepared for the young heir was flung to a fishergirl expecting her base-born baby: the small garments into which Alison had sewn her tears with the stitches went the same road. There was many an honest wife might have had the things, but that would not have pleased the grim humour of the second wife towards the woman she had supplanted.

Everything that had been Alison's was destroyed or hidden away. Her rooms were changed out of all memory of her. There was nothing, nothing in the house to recall to her widower her gentleness, or her face as he had last seen it, snow-pale and pure between the long ashen-fair strands of her hair. He never came upon anything that could give him a tender stab with the thought of her. So she was forgotten, and the man was happy with his children and his beautiful passionate wife, and the constant tenderness with which she surrounded every hour of his life.

Little by little she had won over all who had cause to love the dead woman, all human creatures, that is to say: a dog was more faithful and had resisted her. Alison's dog was a terrier, old, shaggy and blear-eyed: he had been young with his dead mistress, and had seemed to grow old when she died.

The First Wife

He had fretted incessantly during that year of her husband's widowhood, whimpering and moaning about the house like a distraught creature, and following the man in a heavy melancholy when he made his pilgrimages to the grave. He continued those pilgrimages after the man had forgotten, but the heavy iron gate of the Abbey clanged in his face, and since he could not reach the grave his visits grew fewer and fewer. But he had not forgotten.

The new mistress had put out all her fascinations to win the dog too, for it seemed that while any living creature clung to the dead woman's memory her triumph was not complete. But the dog, amenable to every one else, was savage to her. All her soft overtures were received with snarling, and an uncovering of the strong white teeth that was dangerous. The woman was not without a heart, except for the dead, and the misery of the dog moved her—his restlessness, his whining, the channels that tears had worn under his faithful eyes. She would have liked to take him up in her arms and comfort him; but once when her pity moved her to attempt it, the dog ran at her ravening. The husband cried out: "Has he hurt you, my Love?" and was for stringing him up. But some compunction stirred in her, and she saved him from the rope, though she made no more attempts to conciliate him.

After that the dog disappeared from the warm living-rooms, where he had been used to stretch on the rug before the leaping wood-fires. It was a cold and stormy autumn, with many shipwrecks, and mourning in the village for drowned husbands and sons, whose little fishing boats had been sucked into the boiling surges. The roar of the wind and the roar of the waves made a perpetual tumult in the air, and the creaking and lashing of the forest trees aided the wild confusion. There were nights when the crested battalions of the waves stormed the hillsides and foamed over the Abbey graves, and weltered about the hearthstones of the high-perched fishing village.

When there was not storm there was bitter black frost.

The old house had attics in the gables, seldom visited. You went up from the inhabited portions by a corkscrew staircase, steep as a ladder. The servants did not like the attics. There were creaking footsteps on the floors at night, and sometimes the slamming of a door or the stealthy opening of a window. They complained that locked doors up there flew open, and bolted windows were found unbolted. In storm the wind keened like a banshee, and one bright snowy morning a housemaid, who had business there, found a slender wet footprint on the floor as of some one who had come barefoot through the snow; and fled down shrieking.

In one of the attics stood a great hasped chest, wherein the dead woman's dresses were mouldering. The chest was locked, and was likely to remain so for long, for the new mistress had flung away the key. From the high attic windows there was a glorious view of sea and land, of the red sandstone valleys where the deer were feeding, of the black tossing woods, of the roan bulls grazing quietly in the park, and far beyond, of the sea, and the fishing fleet, and in the distance the smoke of a passing steamer. But none observed that view. There was not a servant in the house who would lean from the casement without expecting the touch of a clay-cold finger on her shoulder. Any whose business brought them to the attic looked in the corners warily, while they stayed, but the servants did not like to go there alone. They said the room smelt strangely of earth, and that the air struck with an insidious chill: and a gamekeeper being in full view of the attic window one night declared that from the window came a faint moving glow, and that a wavering shadow moved in the room.

It was in this cold attic the dog took up his abode. He followed a servant up there one morning, and broke out into an excited whimpering when he came near the chest.

After a while of sniffing and rubbing against it he established himself upon it with his nose on his paws. Afterwards he refused to leave it. Finally the servants gave up the attempt to coax him back into the world, and with a compunctious pity they spread an old rug for him on the chest, and fed him faithfully every day. The master never inquired for him: he was glad to have the brute out of his sight: the mistress heard of the fancy which possessed him, and said nothing: she had given up thinking to win him over. So he grew quite old and grizzled, and half blind as summers and winters passed by. It grew a superstition with the servants to take care of him, and with them on their daily visits he was so affectionate and caressing as to recall the days in which some of them remembered him when his mistress lived, and he was a happy dog, as good at fighting and rat-hunting and weasel-catching as any dog in the Island.

But every night as twelve o'clock struck the dog came down the attic stairs. He was suddenly alert and cheerful, and trotted by an invisible gown. Some said you could hear the faint rustle of silk lapping from stair to stair, and the dog would sometimes bark sharply as in his days of puppyhood, and leap up to lick a hand of air. The servants would shut their doors as they heard the patter of the dog's feet coming, and his sudden bark. They were thrilled with a superstitious awe, but they were not afraid the ghost would harm them. They remembered how just, how gentle, how pure the dead woman had been. They whispered that she might well be dreeing this purgatory of returning to her dispossessed house for another's sake, not her own. Husband and wife were nearly always in their own room when she passed. She went everywhere looking to the fastenings of the house, trying every door and window as she had done in the old days, when her husband declared the old place was only precious because it held her. Presently the servants came to look on her guardianship of the house as holy, for one night some careless person had left a light burning where the wind blew the curtains about, and they took fire, and were extinguished, by whom none knew; but in the morning there was the charred curtain, and Molly, the kitchenmaid, confessed with tears how she had forgotten the lighted candle.

The husband was the last of all to hear of these strange doings, for the new wife took care that they should never be about the house at midnight. But one night as he lay in bed he had forgotten something and asked her to fetch it from below. She looked at him with a disdain out of the mists of her black hair, which she was combing to her knee. Perhaps for a minute she resented his unfaithfulness to the dead. "No," she said, with deliberation, "not till that dog and his companion pass." She flung the door open, and looked half with fear, half with defiance, at the black void outside. There was the patter of the dog's feet coming down the stairs swiftly. The man lifted himself on his elbow and listened. Side by side with the dog's feet came the swish, swish of a silken gown on the stairs. He looked a wild-eyed inquiry at his second wife. She slammed the door to before she answered him. "It has been so for years," she said; "every one knew but you. She has not forgotten as easily as you have."

One day the dog died, worn out with age. After that they heard the ghost no longer. Perhaps her purgatory of seeing the second wife in her place was completed, and she was fit for Paradise, or her suffering had sufficed to win another's pardon. From that time the new wife reigned without a rival, living or dead, near her throne.

The Dead Mother

I had been buried a month and a year,
    The clods on my coffin were heavy and brown,
The wreaths at my headstone were withered sere,
    No feet came now from the little town;
I was forgotten, six months or more,
And a new bride walked on my husband's floor.

Below the dew and the grass-blades lying,
    On All Souls' Night, when the moon is cold,
I heard the sound of my children crying,
    And my hands relaxed from their quiet fold;
Through mould and death-damp it pierced my heart,
And I woke in the dark with a sudden start.

I cast the coffin-lid off my face,
    From mouth and eyelids I thrust the clay,
And I stood upright from the sleeper's place,
    And down through the graveyard I took my way.
The frost on the rank grass shimmered like snow,
And the ghostly graves stood white in a row.

As I went down through the little town
    The kindly neighbours seemed sore afeard,
For Lenchen plucked at the cross in her gown,
    And Hans said, "Jesu," under his beard,

The Death Spancel

And many a lonely wayfarer
Crossed himself, with a muttered prayer.

I signed the holy sign on my brows,
    And kissed the crucifix hid in my shroud,
As I reached the door of my husband's house
    The children's clamour rose wild and loud;
And swiftly I came to the upper floor,
And oped, in the moonlight, the nursery door.

No lamp or fire in the icy room;
    'Twas cold, as cold as my bed in the sod.
My two boys fought in that ghostly gloom
    For a mildewed crust that a mouse had gnawed;
"Oh, mother, mother!" my Gretchen said,
"We have been hungry since you were dead."

But what had come to my tender one,
    My babe of little more than a year?
Her limbs were cold as my breast of stone,
    But I hushed her weeping with—"Mother is here."
My children gathered about my knees,
And stroked with soft fingers my draperies.

They did not fear me, my babies sweet.
    I lit the fire in the cheerless stove,
And washed their faces, and hands, and feet,
    And combed the golden fleeces I love,
And brought them food, and drink, and a light,
And tucked them in with a last "Good night."

Then softly, softly I took my way,
    Noiselessly over the creaking stair,
Till I came to the room where their father lay,

The Dead Mother

    And dreamed of his new love's yellow hair;
And I bent and whispered low in his ear,
"Our children were cold and hungry, dear."

Then he awoke with a sob at his heart,
    For he thought of me in the churchyard mould,
And we went together—we, far apart—
    Where our children lay in the moonlight cold;
And he kissed their faces, and wept and said—
"Oh, dead love, rest in your quiet bed.

"To-morrow shall these be warm and glad,
    With food and clothing, and light and wine,
And brave toy-soldiers for each little lad,
    And Gretchen shall nurse a dolly so fine;
But, baby, baby, what shall we do?
For only the mother can comfort you."

I heard the break in his voice, and went—
    'Twould soon be cock-crow; the dawn was near—
And I laid me down with a full content
    That all was well with my children dear;
And my baby came in a month or less—
She was far too young to be motherless.

The Sea's Dead

In Achill it was dreary wet weather—one of innumerable wet summers that blight the potatoes and blacken the hay and mildew the few oats and rot the poor cabin roofs. The air smoked all day with rain mixed with the fine salt spray from the ocean. Out of doors everything shivered and was disconsolate. Only the bog prospered, basking its length in water, and mirroring Croghan and Slievemore with the smoky clouds incessantly wreathing about their foreheads, or drifting like ragged wisps of muslin down their sides to the clustering cabins more desolate than a deserted nest. Inland from the sheer ocean cliffs the place seemed all bog; the little bits of earth the people had reclaimed were washed back into the bog, the grey bents and rimy grasses that alone flourished drank their fill of the water, and were glad. There was a grief and trouble on all the Island. Scarce a cabin in the queer straggling villages but had desolation sitting by its hearth. It was only a few weeks ago that the hooker had capsized crossing to Westport, and the famine that is always stalking ghost-like in Achill was forgotten in the contemplation of new graves. The Island was full of widows and orphans and bereaved old people; there was scarce a window sill in Achill by which the banshee had not cried.

Where all were in trouble there were few to go about with comfort. Moya Lavelle shut herself up in the cabin her husband Patrick had built, and dreed her weird alone. Of all the boys who had gone down with the hooker none was finer than Patrick Lavelle. He was brown and handsome, broad-shouldered and clever, and he had the good-humoured smile and the kindly word where the people are normally taciturn and unsmiling. The Island girls were disappointed when Patrick brought a wife from the mainland, and Moya never tried to make friends with them. She was something of a mystery to the Achill people, this small moony creature, with her silver fair hair, and strange light eyes, the colour of spilt milk. She was as small as a child, but had the gravity of a woman. She loved the sea with a love unusual in Achill, where the sea is to many a ravening monster that has exacted in return for its hauls of fish the life of husband and son. Patrick Lavelle had built for her a snug cabin in a sheltered ravine. A little beach ran down in front of it where he could haul up his boat. The cabin was built strongly, as it had need to be, for often of a winter night the waves tore against its little windows. Moya loved the fury of the elements, and when the winter storms drove the Atlantic up the ravine with a loud bellowing, she stirred in sleep on her husband's shoulder, and smiled as they say children smile in sleep when an angel leans over them.

Higher still, on a spur of rock, Patrick Lavelle had laid the clay for his potatoes. He had carried it on his shoulders, every clod, and Moya had gathered the seaweed to fertilise it. She had her small garden there, too, of sea-pinks and the like, which rather encouraged the Islanders in their opinion of her strangeness. In Achill the struggle for life is too keen to admit of any love for mere beauty.

However, Patrick Lavelle was quite satisfied with his little wife. When he came home from the fishing he found his cabin more comfortable than is often the case in Achill. They had no child, but Moya never seemed to miss a child's head at her breast. During the hours of his absence at the fishing she seemed to find the sea sufficient company. She was always roaming along the cliffs, gazing down as with a fearful fascination along the black sides to where the waves churned hundreds of feet below. For company she had only the seagulls and the bald eagle that screamed far over her head; but she was quite happy as she roamed hither and thither, gathering the coloured seaweeds out of the clefts of the rocks, and crooning an old song softly to herself, as a child might do.

But that was all over and gone, and Moya was a widow. She had nothing warm and human at all, now that brave protecting tenderness was gone from her. No one came to the little cabin in the ravine where Moya sat and moaned, and stretched her arms all day for the dear brown head she had last seen stained with the salt water and matted with the seaweeds. At night she went out, and wandered moon-struck by the black cliffs, and cried out for Patrick, while the shrilling gusts of wind blew her pale hair about her, and scourged her fevered face with the sea salt and the sharp hail.

One night a great wave broke over Achill. None had seen it coming, with great crawling leaps like a serpent, but at dead of night it leaped the land, and hissed on the cottage hearths and weltered grey about the mud floors. The next day broke on ruin in Achill. The bits of fields were washed away, the little mountain sheep were drowned, the cabins were flung in ruined heaps; but the day was fair and sunny, as if the elements were tired of the havoc they had wrought and were minded to be in a good humour. There was not a boat on the Island but had been battered and torn by the rocks. People had to take their heads out of their hands, and stand up from their brooding, or this wanton mischief would cost them their dear lives, for the poor resources of the Island had given out, and the Islanders were in grips with starvation.

No one thought of Moya Lavelle in her lonely cabin in the ravine. None knew of the feverish vigils in those wild nights.

But a day or two later the sea washed her on a stretch of beach to the very doors of a few straggling cabins dotted here and there beyond the irregular village. She had been carried out to sea that night, but the sea, though it had snatched her to itself, had not battered and bruised her. She lay there, indeed, like that blessed Restituta, whom, for her faith, the tyrant sent bound on a rotting hulk, with the outward tide from Carthage, to die on the untracked ocean. She lay like a child smiling in dreams, all her long silver hair about her, and her wide eyes gazing with no such horror, as of one who meets a violent death. Those who found her so wept to behold her.

They carried her to her cottage in the ravine, and waked her. Even in Achill they omit no funeral ceremony. They dressed her in white and put a cross in her hand, and about her face on the pillow they set the sea-pinks from her little garden, and some of the coloured seaweeds she had loved to gather. They lit candles at her head and feet, and the women watched with her all day, and at night the men came in, and they talked and told stories, subdued stories and ghostly, of the banshee and the death-watch, and wraiths of them gone that rise from the sea to warn fishermen of approaching death. Gaiety there was none: the Islanders had no heart for gaiety: but the pipes and tobacco were there, and the plate of snuff, and the jar of poteen to lift up the heavy hearts. And Moya lay like an image wrought of silver, her lids kept down by coins over her blue eyes.

She had lain so two nights, nights of starlit calm. On the fourth day they were to bury her beside Patrick Lavelle in his narrow house, and the little bridal cabin would be abandoned, and presently would rot to ruins. The third night had come, overcast with heavy clouds. The group gathered in the death chamber was more silent than before. Some had sat up the two nights, and were now dazed with sleep. By the wall the old women nodded over their beads, and a group of men talked quietly at the bed-head where Moya lay illumined by the splendour of the four candles all shining on her white garments.

Suddenly in the quietness there came a roar of wind. It did not come freshening from afar off, but seemed to waken suddenly in the ravine and cry about the house. The folk sprang to their feet startled, and the eyes of many turned towards the little dark window, expecting to see wild eyes and a pale face set in black hair gazing in. Some who were nearest saw in the half-light for it was whitening towards day a wall of grey water travelling up the ravine. Before they could cry a warning it had encompassed the house, had driven door and window before it, and the living and the dead were in the sea.

The wave retreated harmlessly, and in a few minutes the frightened folk were on their feet amid the wreck of stools and tables floating. The wave that had beaten them to earth had extinguished the lights. When they stumbled to their feet and got the water out of their eyes the dim dawn was in the room. They were too scared for a few minutes to think of the dead. When they recovered and turned towards the bed there was a simultaneous loud cry. Moya Lavelle was gone. The wave had carried her away, and never more was there tale or tidings of her body.

Achill people said she belonged to the sea, and the sea had claimed her. They remembered Patrick Lavelle's silence as to where he had found her. They remembered a thousand unearthly ways in her; and which of them had ever seen her pray? They pray well in Achill, having a sure hold on that heavenly country which is to atone for the cruelty and sorrow of this. In process of time they will come to think of her as a mermaid, poor little Moya. She had loved her husband at least with a warm human love. But his open grave was filled after they had given up hoping that the sea would again give her up, and the place by Patrick Lavelle's side remains for ever empty.

The Dead Tryst

As I went by the harbour when folk were abed
    I saw my dead lover in the boat pulling in;
My love he came swiftly and kissed my whitening head,
    And my cheeks so hollow and thin.

And face to face we nestled by the wash of the foam,
    And after long sorrow the joy it was sweet.
I combed his locks of honey with my little silver comb,
    And with my hands I warmed his feet.

The sea fog crept round us as white as the wool.
    And he lay on the sea sand with his head on my knee,
No night wind broke the silence, nor any shrieking gull,
    In that death white fog from the sea.

And then I crooned him over our sweet songs of old;
    Ochone, I could not warm him, and never a word he spoke.
I loosed my head hair then, the grey locks with the gold,
    And wrapped him in a living cloak.

I never thought to ask him the wherefore he had come.
    Or if his heaven were lonely and this earth so dear;
I prayed with eager longing that the cocks would be dumb,
    And the nighttime last a year.

The Death Spancel

Ochone, the cocks came crowing, and he arose and went,
   His darling black head hanging, out through the sea fog's snow.
Oh, wherefore, darling, darling, did you break my full content,
   And why did you come but to go?

The Death Spancel

High up among the dusty rafters of Aughagree Chapel dangles a thin shrivelled thing, towards which the people look shudderingly when the sermon is of the terrors of the Judgment and the everlasting fire. The woman from whose dead body that was taken chose the death of the soul in return for a life with the man whom she loved with an unholy passion. Every man, woman, and child in that chapel amid grey miles of rock and sea-drift, has heard over and over of the unrepentant deathbed of Mauryeen Holion. They whisper on winter nights of how Father Hugh fought with the demons for her soul, how the sweat poured from his forehead, and he lay on his face in an agony of tears, beseeching that the sinner whom he had admitted into the fold of Christ should yet be saved. But of her love and her sin she had no repentance, and the servants in Rossatorc Castle said that as the priest lay exhausted from his vain supplications, and the rattle was in Dark Mauryeen's throat, there were cries of mocking laughter in the air above the castle, and a strange screaming and flapping of great wings, like to, but incomparably greater than, the screaming and flapping of the eagle over Slieve League. That devil's charm up there in the rafters of Aughagree is the death-spancel by which Dark Mauryeen bound Sir Robert Molyneux to her love. It is of such power that no man born of woman can resist it, save by the power of the Cross, and 'twas little Robert Molyneux of Rossatorc recked of the sweet Christ who perished that men should live—against whose Cross the demons of earth and the demons of air, the malevolent spirits that lurk in water and wind, and all witches and evil doctors, are powerless. But the thought of the death-spancel must have come straight from the King of Fiends himself, for who else would harden the human heart to desecrate a new grave, and to cut from the helpless dead the strip of skin unbroken from head to heel which is the death-spancel? Very terrible is the passion of love when it takes full possession of a human heart, and no surer weapon to the hand of Satan when he would make a soul his own. And there is the visible sign of a lost soul, and it had nearly been of two, hanging harmlessly in the rafters of the holy place. A strange thing to see where the lamp of the sanctuary burns, and the sea-wind sighs sweetly through the door ever open for the continual worshippers.

Sir Robert Molyneux was a devil-may-care, sporting squire, with the sins of his class to his account. He drank, and gambled, and rioted, and oppressed his people that they might supply his pleasures; nor was that all, for he had sent the daughter of honest people in shame and sorrow over the sea. People muttered when they heard he was to marry Lord Dunlough's daughter, that she would be taking another woman's place; but it was said yet again that it would be well for his tenants when he was married, for the lady was so kind and charitable, so gentle and pure, that her name was loved for many a mile. She had never heard the shameful story of that forlorn girl sailing away and away in the sea-mist, with her unborn child, to perish miserably, body and soul, in the streets of New York. She had the strange love of a pure woman for a wild liver; and she thought fondly when she caressed his fine, jolly, handsome face that soon his soul as

The Death Spancel

well as his dear body would be in her keeping: and what safe keeping it would be.

Sir Robert had ever a free way with women of a class below his own, and he did not find it easy to relinquish it. When he was with the Lady Eva he felt that under those innocent, loving eyes a man could have no desire for a lesser thing than her love; but when he rode away, the first pretty girl he met on the road he held in chat that ended with a kiss. He was always for kissing a pretty face, and found the habit hard to break, though there were times when he stamped and swore great oaths to himself that he would again kiss no woman's lips but his wife's—for the man had the germ of good in him.

It was a fortnight to his wedding day, and he had had a hard day's hunting. From early morning to dewy eve they had been at it, for the fox was an old one and had led the dogs many a dance before this. He turned homeward with a friend, splashed and weary, but happy and with the appetite of a hunter. Well for him if he had never set foot in that house. As he came down the stairs fresh and shining from his bath, he caught sight of a girl's dark handsome face on the staircase. She was one of the servants, and she stood aside to let him pass, but that was never Robert Molyneux's way with a woman. He flung his arm round her waist in a way so many poor girls had found irresistible. For a minute or two he looked in her dark splendid eyes; but then as he bent lightly to kiss her, she tore herself from him with a cry and ran away into the darkness.

He slept heavily that night, the dead sleep of a man who has hunted all day and has drunk deep in the evening. In the morning he awoke sick and sorry, a strange mood for Robert Molyneux; but from midnight to dawn he had lain with the death-spancel about his knees. In the blackness of his mind he had a great longing for the sweet woman, his love for whom awakened all that was good in him. His horse had fallen lame, but after breakfast he asked his host to order out a carriage that he might go to her. Once with her he thought all would be well. Yet as he stood on the doorstep he had a strange reluctance to go.

It was a drear, grey, miserable day, with sleet pattering against the carriage windows. Robert Molyneux sat with his head bent almost to his knees, and his hands clenched. What face was it rose against his mind, continually blotting out the fair and sweet face of his love? It was the dark, handsome face of the woman he had met on the stairs last night. Some sudden passion for her rose as strong as hell-fire in his breast. There were many long miles between him and Eva, and his desire for the dark woman raged stronger and ever stronger in him. It was as if ropes were around his heart dragging it backward. He fell on his knees in the carriage, and sobbed. If he had known how to pray he would have prayed, for he was torn in two between the desire of his heart for the dark woman, and the longing of his soul for the fair woman. Again and again he started up to call the coachman to turn back; again and again he flung himself in the bottom of the carriage, and hid his face and struggled with the curse that had come upon him. And every mile brought him nearer to Eva and safety.

The coachman drove on in the teeth of the sleet and wondered what Sir Robert would give him at the drive's end. A half-sovereign would not be too much for so open-handed a gentleman, and one so near his wedding; and the coachman, already feeling his hand close upon it, turned a brave face to the sleet and tried not to think of the warm fire in the harness-room from which they had called him to drive Sir Robert.

Half the distance was gone when he heard a voice from the carriage window calling him. He turned round. "Back! Back!" said the voice. "Drive like hell! I will give you a sovereign if you do it under an hour." The coachman was amazed, but a sovereign is better than a half-sovereign. He turned his bewildered horses for home.

Robert Molyneux's struggle was over. Eva's face was gone now altogether. He only felt a mad joy in yielding, and a wild desire for the minutes to pass till he had traversed that grey road back. The coachman drove hard and his horses were flecked with foam, but from the windows Robert Molyneux kept continually urging him, offering him greater and greater rewards for his doing the journey with all speed.

Half way up the cypress avenue to his friend's house a woman with a shawl about her head glided from the shadow and signalled to the darkly flushed face at the carriage window. Robert Molyneux shouted to the man to stop. He sprang from the carriage and lifted the woman in. Then he flung the coachman a handful of gold and silver. "To Rossatorc," he said, and the man turned round and once more whipped up his tired horses. The woman laughed as Robert Molyneux caught her in his arms. It was the fierce laughter of the lost. "I came to meet you," she said, "because I knew you must come."

From that day, when Robert Molyneux led the woman over the threshold of his house, he was seen no more in the usual places of his fellow-men. He refused to see any one who came. His wedding-day passed by. Lord Dunlough had ridden furiously to have an explanation with the fellow and to horsewhip him when that was done, but he found the great door of Rossatorc closed in his face. Every one knew Robert Molyneux was living in shame with Mauryeen Holion. Lady Eva grew pale and paler, and drooped and withered in sorrow and shame, and presently her father took her away, and their house was left to servants. Burly neighbouring squires rode up and knocked with their riding-whips at Rossatorc door to remonstrate with Robert Molyneux, for his father's sake or for his own, but met no answer. All the servants were gone except a furtive-eyed French valet and a woman he called his wife, and these were troubled with no notions of respectability. After a time people gave up trying to interfere. The place got a bad name. The gardens were neglected and the house was half in ruins. No one ever saw Mauryeen Holion's face except it might be at a high window of the castle, when some belated huntsman taking a short-cut across the park would catch a glimpse of a wild face framed in black hair at an upper window, the flare of the winter sunset lighting it up, it might be, as with a radiance from hell. Sir Robert drank, they said, and rack-rented his people far worse than in the old days. He had put his business in the hands of a disreputable attorney from a neighbouring town, and if the rent was not paid to the day the roof was torn off the cabin, and the people flung out into the ditch to rot.

So the years went, and folk ever looked for a judgment of God on the pair. And when many years were over, there came to Father Hugh, wringing her hands, the wife of the Frenchman, with word that the two were dying, and she dared not let them die in their sins.

But Mauryeen Holion, Dark Mauryeen, as they called her, would not to her last breath yield up the death-spancel which she had knotted round her waist, and which held Robert Molyneux's love to her. When the wicked breath was out of her body they cut it away, and it lay twisted on the ground like a dead snake. Then on Robert Molyneux, dying in a distant chamber, came a strange peace. All the years of sin seemed blotted out, and he was full of a simple repentance such as he had felt long ago when kneeling by the gown of the good woman whom he had loved. So Father Hugh absolved him before he died, and went hither and thither through the great empty rooms shaking his holy water, and reading from his Latin book.

And lest any in that place, where they have fiery southern blood in their veins, should so wickedly use philtres or charms, he hung the death-spancel in Aughagree Chapel for a terrible reminder.

The Death-Watch

Ullagone! Ullagone!
He and I were all alone.
In the wall by the thatch
I heard the tick of the death-watch.

Ullagone! Ullagone!
And my heart grew cold as stone:
Tick, tick, all was still
Save that ghastly note of ill.

On the flaring candle grew
Plain an awful shape I knew:
Tick, tick, in the thatch
Went the beat of the death-watch.

Ullagone! Ullagone!
And the tide went with a moan.
Bring the candles, two and three;
Chant the dead man's litany.

Strew the rose, the rosemary gather
For the husband and the father:
Tick, tick, in the thatch
Hear the knell of the death-watch!

The Ghosts

We were very old-fashioned at Aghadoe Abbey and satisfied with old-fashioned ways. There was a great deal of talk about opening up the country, and even the gentry were full of it, but my grandfather would take snuff and look scornful.

"And when you have opened it up," he said, "you will let in the devil and all his angels."

It was certainly true that the people had hitherto been kind and innocent, so that any change might be for the worse, yet I was a little curious about what lay out in the world beyond our hills. And now it was no great journey to see, for they had opened a light railway, and from the front of the house we could see beyond the lake and the park, through the opening where the Purple Hill rises, that weird thing which rushes round the base of the hill half a dozen times a day before it climbs with no effort to the gorge between the hills and makes its way into the world. It does not even go by steam, so the thing was a great marvel to us and our people, to whom steam was quite marvel enough.

My grandfather at first would not even look on it. I have seen him turn away sharply from the window to avoid seeing it. When we went out to drive we turned our backs upon it, my grandfather saying that he would not insult his horses by letting them look at it, and indeed I think that, old as they were, yet having blood in them they would curvet a bit if they saw anything so strange to them.

There is one thing the light railway has done, and that is to give the people a market for their goods. We were all much poorer than we once were, except Mr. Dawson, who made his money by money-lending in Dublin and London; but even with Mr. Dawson's big house we did not make a market for the countryside.

Besides, there was a stir among the people there used not to be. They were spinning and weaving in their cottages, and they were rearing fowl and growing fruit and flowers.

The things which before the peasant children did for sport they now did for profit as well. It caused the greatest surprise in the minds of the people when they discovered that anybody could want their blackberries and their mushrooms; that money was to be made out of even the gathering of shamrocks. They thought that people out in the world who were ready to pay money for such things must be very queer people indeed. But since there were "such quare ould oddities", it was just as well, since they made life easier for the poor.

Another thing was that a creamery had been started at Araglin, only a mile or two from us, and the girls went there from the farms to learn the trade of dairying.

If it were not for the light railway none of these things would have been possible, and so I forgave it that it flew with a shriek round the base of the Purple Hill, setting all the mountains rattling with echoes, and disturbing the water fowl on the lakes and the songbirds in the woods, the eagle in his eyrie, and the wild red deer, to say nothing of the innumerable grouse and partridges and black cock and plover and hares and rabbits on the mountain-side.

My grandmother was not as angry against the light railway as my grandfather; she used to say that we must go with the times, and she was glad the people were stirring since it kept their thoughts from turning to America. She had been talked over by Miss Champion, my godmother and the greatest friend we have. And Miss Champion was always on the side of the people, and had even persuaded my grandmother to let her have some of her famous recipes, such as those for elder and blackberry wine, and for various preserves, and for fine soaps and washes for the skin, so that the people might know them and make more money.

"Every one makes money except the gentry," my grandfather grumbled, "and we grow poorer year by year."

My grandfather talked freely in my presence; and I knew that Aghadoe Abbey was mortgaged to the doors and that the mortgages would be foreclosed at my grandfather's death. They kept nothing from me, and my grandmother has said to me with a watery smile: "If I survive your grandfather, Bawn, my dear, you and I will have to find genteel lodgings in Dublin. It would be a strange thing for a Lady St. Leger to come down from Aghadoe Abbey to that. To be sure there was once a Countess went ballad-singing in the streets of Cork."

"That day is far away," I answered. "And when it comes there will be no genteel lodgings, but Theobald and I will take care of you somewhere. In a little house it may be, but one with a garden where you can walk in the sun in winter mornings as you do now, and prod at the weeds in the path as you do now with your silver-headed cane."

"If I could survive your grandfather," she said, turning away her head, "my heart would break to leave Aghadoe. I ask nothing of you and Theobald, Bawn, but that you should take care of each other when we are gone. It is not right that the old should burden the young."

I have always known, or at least since I was capable of entertaining such things, that our grandparents destined Theobald and me for each other. I have no love for Theobald such as I find in my books, but I have a great affection for him as the dearest of brothers.

I have not said before that he is a soldier. What else should he be but a soldier? Since there have always been soldiers in the family, and my grandfather could not have borne him to be anything else.

Dear Theobald, how brave and simple and kind he was!

I have said nothing about the ghosts of Aghadoe Abbey, but it has many ghosts, or it had.

First and foremost there is the Lord St. Leger, who was killed in a Dublin street brawl a hundred years ago, who will come driving home at midnight headless in his coach, and the coachman driving him also headless, carrying his head under his arm. That is not a very pleasant thing to see enter as the gates swing open of themselves to let the ghost through.

Then there is the ghost of the woman who cries outside in the shrubbery. I have seen her myself in a glint of the moonlight, her black hair covering her face as she bends to the earth, incessantly seeking something among the dead leaves, which she cannot discover, and for which she cries.

And again, there is the lady who goes down the stairs, down, down, through the underground passage, and yet lower to the well that lies under the house, and is seen no more. A new maid once saw her in broad daylight—or at least in the grey of the morning—and followed her down the stairs, thinking that it was one of the family ill perhaps, who needed some attention. She could tell afterwards the very pattern of the lace on the fine nightgown, and describe how the fair curls clustered on the lady's neck. It was only when the lady disappeared before her, a white shimmer down the darkness of the underground corridor, that the poor thing realised she had seen a ghost, and fell fainting, with a clatter of her dustpan and brush which brought her help.

I could make a long list of the ghosts, for they are many, but I will not, lest I should be tedious. Only Aghadoe Abbey was eerie at night, especially in winter storms, since my cousin

Theobald went away. I have often thought that the curious formation of the house, which has as many rooms beneath the ground as above it, helped to give it an eerie feeling, for one could not but imagine those downstairs rooms filled with ghosts. I had seen the rooms lit dimly once or twice, but for a long time we had not used them, the expense of lighting them with a thousand wax candles glimmering in glittering chandeliers being too great.

But in the days before Cousin Theobald left us I was not afraid. He slept across the corridor from my room, and I had only to cry out and I knew he would fly to my assistance.

His sword was new at that time, and he was very proud of it. He turned it about, making it flash in the sunlight, and, said he, "Cousin Bawn, fear nothing; for if anything were to frighten you, either ghost or mortal, I would run it through with my sword. At your least cry I should wake, and I have always the sword close to my hand. Very often I lie awake when you do not think it to watch over you."

It gave me great comfort at the time, though looking back on it now I think my cousin, being so healthy and in the air all day, must have slept very soundly. Yet I am sure he thought he woke.

And, indeed, after he left the ghosts were worse than ever. I used to take my little dog into my arms for company, and, hiding my head under the bedclothes, I used to lie quaking because of the crying of the ghosts. It was a wild winter when Theobald left us, and they cried every night. It is a sound I have never grown used to, though I have heard it every winter I can remember. And also the swish of the satin as it went by my door, and the tap of high-heeled shoes. They cried more that winter than I ever heard them, except in the winter after Uncle Luke went away (but then I was little, and had the company of Maureen Kelly, my nurse); and in a winter which was yet to be.

But at that time I was happy despite the ghosts, and had no idea that the world held any fate for me other than to be always among such gentle, high-minded people as were my grandfather and grandmother, my cousin Theobald, and my dear godmother. For ghosts, especially of one's own blood, are gentle and little likely to harm one, and must be permitted by the good God to come back for some good reason.

It is another matter when it is some one of flesh and blood, who wants to take you in his arms and kiss you while your flesh creeps, and your whole soul cries out against it. And it is the worst matter of all when those to whom you have fled all your days for help and protection, to whom you would have looked to save you from such a thing, look on, with pale faces indeed, yet never interfere.

Often, often in the days that were to come I had rather be of the company of the ghosts than to endure the things I had to endure.

A Bride from the Dead

It was in the year of the Great comet that Terence L'Estrange met with a strange adventure.

He was a golden youth at College in that year, much given to all sorts of diversion. He would dance three nights of the week and sit up at a spree the other three, and not show a trace of it the next day at lecture or in the class-room; and he was always ready for sport when the working hours were over, and you might have supposed that he'd be only too glad to get to his bed and have a sleep. But Terry L'Estrange would have said that you couldn't waste your time more than in sleeping: there would be plenty of time to sleep when he was old, a time which seemed to Terry L'Estrange as removed as the Conversion of the Jews.

He was a handsome, golden-haired lad, with a touch of the gold in his clear skin, laughing blue eyes and a coaxing tongue. He was so entirely youthful and debonair, so full of the joy of life, that he made weary people sigh and smile to look at him. And he was a dog with the girls. He couldn't help making love to every girl he met; but the way he did it was so gay, so audacious, so irresistible, that he left no sore hearts behind him. It wasn't in him to hurt anyone if he could help it, much less a girl, and he was fond of all girls.

It was at a dance at Kiltrasna Abbey that he got left behind when the other youths went back in the brake to College. He had forgotten the time, sitting in some quiet corner with a girl: and when the hue and cry failed to find him it was only a joke to the other boys to leave him to walk the five miles back to College.

It was an intensely dark night, full of stars and very cold, when Terry L'Estrange set out to walk the five miles, jovially anathematising the other fellows who had gone off without him.

"A fine night for the Comet," someone called after him as he started away from Kiltrasna, his coat-collar up about his ears and his hands thrust deep in his pockets for warmth.

It was indeed a splendid night for the Comet. There it was blazing away low down in the south-west, with the tail of it, like the reflection of a flash-light, high in the air. As he walked, the frozen leaves crackled under his feet. He began to be conscious of fatigue; and it came to him with something of a shock that he had an exam the next day. It was strange to him to have the sensation of being heavy-handed and heavy-eyed; but he hadn't had a night in bed for a week, and it began to tell on him.

He walked along doggedly in the shade of Belview wall, which by-and-by hid the Comet from his sight. It was pitch-black under the high wall and the trees. Terry didn't know what it was to be afraid of anything, but he acknowledged to himself that if he had the capacity for fear he might have been frightened when he fell over an old donkey in the shadow of the wall, and again when a chain's rattling resolved itself into an old goat broken loose from her tether and trailing it along the ground after her as she went.

He had to pass by the Kiltrasna Churchyard, a lonely place of the dead, behind high walls, grass-over-grown, with only the ruined gable of an ancient church to keep watch and ward among the graves. Another time he would not have thought about the graveyard. There were many such scattered over the country. But to-night one of his pretty partners had suddenly sighed, and grown a little pale.

"The last time I was here," she had said: "the prettiest girl—we all gave it to her—was Sheila O'Connell, and to-night she's in her grave in Kitrasna. Only this morning they buried her."

It gave him a grue as he passed under the churchyard wall. The thought of the prettiest face at the ball lying there so cold, with the coffin-lid above it, and the earth pressing on that, made his heart suddenly bleed as though he had known and loved the dead girl.

It was too dark to see anything as he passed the wicket gate of the churchyard, or he might have seen that it stood open. He hurried on, colder than before, feeling numbed and sleepy. Fast as he walked he did not seem to get warm. The sense of fatigue which had come upon him made him feel as though he walked in his sleep. He longed for his eyrie at the top of the College, and his own bed, an uncomfortable couch which usually had few attractions for him.

It might have been half a mile from Kiltrasna, and the Comet, low down now, was blazing towards its setting, when—it must have been by the light of the Comet he saw it—he was aware of an old lumbering coach rolling along before him on the Dublin Road.

The sight spurred him. He came up with it as quickly as he could and hailed the driver.

"I'll give you all the money about me, and that's not very much," he said, "if you'll give me a lift on my way. If you go as far as the College it'll be worth five shillings."

There were two men on the box. One muttered what was apparently a curt refusal: but the other looked at Terry L'Estrange by the light of a lucifer match he had struck and held shaded in the hollow of his hand. He measured his height and size.

"If you'll promise to stand by us and speak for us," he said, "in case we're stopped by the new police, we'll give you a lift. A young gentleman of the College—"

"I know every man of the police," said Terry L'Estrange, his hand on the door-handle of the coach.

If you'll promise to stick your head out of the window and speak for us if we're stopped we'll take you as far as we're going. That's not as far as the College, but it's within the bridges. You needn't pay us anything if you'll do us this service."

"An easy one," said Terry L'Estrange.

"As a matter of fact," said the other, bending down and whispering, "it's an elopement. My friend here—you understand. It would be ruin if we were stopped. We had a lie prepared, but a clumsy one. Your word will be better."

"But the lady?"

"The lady is sound asleep in the carriage. You will not disturb her. Poor soul, she is worn out with many emotions. You are a gentleman or we would not trust you. Come, step in."

Terence L'Estrange hesitated. What was this strange story of the sleeping lady and the elopement? The man who had spoken to him was young and evidently a man of education. The other was older, as Terry had perceived in the dim flare of the match. He looked dark and gloomy—not at all like a bridegroom about to be. Plainly he fidgeted with impatience while the brief colloquy lasted.

The mystery tempted Terry L'Estrange beyond his fatigue. A lady—he would see it through—see what they were up to. Some villainy, perhaps. And they expected him, Terry L'Estrange, to assist them in it. Well, he would see.

He turned the door-handle of the coach, and, with a muttered apology, although he had been told the lady slept, he stepped inside. He felt rather than saw the hooded, cloaked figure in the corner of the carriage. He stepped gingerly, to avoid waking her; took the front seat of the carriage, which was wide and roomy out of the common. From where he sat he could see the Comet dimming before it went out.

The roads were rough and full of deep ruts after the winter. The coach, rumbling along, jolted badly, and Terry L'Estrange felt rather than saw that the sleeping figure opposite to him rolled uneasily from side to side. He hoped she would not awake and find a stranger sitting there in the darkness to terrify her. Poor soul! It had not been fair to her to put him where he was. He might as well have sat out with the driver, and the other—the lover, the husband, Terry L'Estrange found an odd incongruity in the thought—have come inside.

They crossed the first of the bridges without mishap, and now they were in the lighted streets. There were only oil lamps that lent a flickering illumination to things in their immediate neighbourhood. Something in the attitude of the figure as revealed by the street lamps struck Terry L'Estrange oddly. Why, she was unconscious, poor soul, not asleep! He caught a glimpse of a pale cheek, of golden hair. What foul play was there here?

He moved quickly to her side. There was something wrong. This was not sleep, but insensibility. The motionless form, the unbreathing lips, the helplessness of the head that wagged this way and that as the carriage jolted, told him that it was not sleep.

They were now in a congeries of little and ill-lightened streets. He wondered what he should do. The thing that commanded itself most to his mind was to summon the first street patrol he saw.

Suddenly the head drooped on his shoulder. The golden hair brushed his cheek. A shock ran through him. The hair was cold, cold and rigid—not warm, living hair. The cheek touched his own. It was frozen. All of a sudden he remembered what his partner in the dance had said. This was a dead girl, and the men he had promised to shield were grave-robbers. He remembered now the darkly anxious face of the other man on the box, and where he had seen it before. Dr. Abrahams, was it? He was the head of one of the Dublin medical schools. Some of the young men swore by him, saying that the passion of his life was for science.

The dead girl's head drooped lower and lay on Terence L'Estrange's shoulder as though it were glad of a resting-place. Some curious, melting tenderness came upon the boy. He was not at all afraid. He looked down at the still face, illumined now and again by a street lamp. It was beautiful in death. There was a scent of flowers, a sensation of flowers crushed against him. The girl had been buried with a pall of flowers, as his partner had told him, and lifting her from the coffin they had taken the flowers with her.

Now, all of a sudden, the greatest pity and despair seized on Terence L'Estrange, as though his heart bled in his breast. That anything so fair, so sweet, should be given to the darkness, the corruption, of the grave! He remembered in his classics the tale of a youth who had fallen in love with the dead. Had the same lonely and terrible thing come to him, that his joyous youth was over, that his manhood was awakened—for a dead girl? What malicious fate had held in store such a tragedy for one as harmless as he?

There was a clatter of horses' hoofs on the cobbles of which the steep little street down which they were going—the mounted police!

Now was his time to give up the miscreants who had robbed the grave in the interests of science—the ghouls, the vampires, who would use so exquisite a piece of human flesh to wrest from it the secrets of life and death! Would nothing baser suffice them?

Then his mood changed. He thought she was warm in his arms. Could he send her back to the grave, to the coldness and the loneliness, and the coffin-lid hiding all that beauty?

The police stopped, crying a halt. They flashed the lanterns they carried on to the coach. Terence L'Estrange thrust out his head. The lantern light flashed on his face.

"Good night, Mr. L'Estrange," said the sergeant of police.

"Good night, sergeant," said Terence. "A fine night for the Comet."

"You ought to be in your bed, sir," said the sergeant in a friendly voice, "and not to be talkin' about the Comet this hour of the mornin'."

"Sure I'm going there as fast as I can," said Terence. "Did you never stay up late at a dance yourself, sergeant?"

"Many's the time, sir. Good night!"

Terence L'Estrange dropped back into his seat with a sense as though he had escaped some terrible danger as the coach rolled on its way. Again the dead girl's head lay as if in sleep upon his shoulder. He stretched out a hand and felt for hers and took it. It was icy cold, but it was not rigid. He took it and fondled it in his own. He felt as though he could hear his own heart dropping blood in the silence and darkness. He was so conscious of that desire to call her back from the dead that it was as though every nerve in him fought with an invisible foe. His soul seemed as though it struggled with invisible powers: pulses beat in his head and his side. He seemed possessed of a superhuman energy—such energy as he must have if he was to fight Death for his prey.

The coach turned clumsily round a corner. The horses slipped and slid on greasy cobble-stones and stood still. The night was giving way to a troubled greyness as Terence L'Estrange looked out. The man he had taken for Dr. Abrahams stood by the coach door. They were at what looked like a stable. Beside the wide doors there was a narrow one which the man who had driven the coach pushed open. Some one came out and stood at the horses' heads.

Dr. Abrahams, if it was he, said in a low voice to Terence L'Estrange:

"We are much obliged to you, sir. If I can do anything to show my indebtedness, I will do it. Hateful necessity that the law forces us to if we would not fight death and pain with an empty armoury! I fear you will think that we played you a trick."

"Let me," said Terence L'Estrange, preventing the man who had driven the coach, as he would have opened its door. "Let me carry her, the poor soul!"

He was taller and stronger than either of the two. He stepped into the coach, lifted the dead girl in his arms, and carried her out.

"Show me the way," he said.

One went before, one went behind, as they passed through the postern door, which was locked and bolted behind them. There was the sound of the horses struggling for foothold on the greasy cobble-stones, the rumbling of the coach as it turned round and went off. They went along what seemed a narrow passage in the dark. The air struck chilly and damp; but Terence L'Estrange was only conscious of the strange sad scent of the crushed flowers which had lain about the dead girl.

A door opened, and a glimmer of light came out. There were many lamps in the room, turned low. The man who had driven the coach, who now revealed himself as a youth no older than Terence L'Estrange, with dark, curly hair, and bright eyes, turned up the lamps. Terence came to a stop in the middle of the room, still holding his burden. There were many things in the long room; but he was only aware of the tables that ran down the middle. Two tables were occupied—with something that showed rigidly under a sheet. There was a drip-drip of falling water. Standing there, with the dead girl in his arms, Terence L'Estrange was aware of the most dreadful repulsion for, and horror of, the place.

"Lay her here!" said Dr. Abrahams, indicating the empty table, "and let us get out of this. Some hot whiskey will not be amiss."

Terence L'Estrange looked at the table. It was not a table he perceived now, but a stone slab hollowed in the middle to a shape which made his blood run cold. There was a strange, heavy, bitter smell in the place. He glanced towards the rigid forms lying under the sheets; then down at the burden he held. A strand of golden hair had escaped from the wrappings and clung to his hand as though these were piteous little fingers clutching him to avert a doom.

"What place is this?" he asked, still holding her as though he could not give her up.

"The dissecting-room of the Grace Dieu Hospital. Allow me to tell you how sorry I am for drawing you into our doings to-night. Believe me, I abhor the necessity. Only my love for science and my kind enables me to go through with such atrocities. Some time I shall be caught and sentenced, if the law is not soon amended. Madden here knows how I sicken at it. He indicated the dark young man. "Scoundrel, to tell you such a story of an elopement! Do I look like a lover? Poor child! Put her down and let us go to my room."

Terence L'Estrange looked at the slab and its terrible hollowed centre. Was she to lie there alone with the dead while he went back to life? He started, with a feeling that something had sighed at his ear, though he knew it was nothing but a delusion.

"I do not believe she is dead," he said, still holding her.

"My dear fellow—we have given you a shock." The haggard face looked at him with anxious kindness. "Put her down and let us leave this place! I daresay it is rather horrible to you, who are not accustomed to it."

"I am sure she is not dead," Terence L'Estrange repeated, with a strange persistency. "See—her hand! Are the hands of dead people flexible like that?"

He lifted the hand, where it lay like a snowflake on his palm, and looked at the other man with an eager expression.

"Oh, yes. That flexibility is, alas, not conclusive. Let me have a look at her."

"Not there," Terence L'Estrange said with quiet violence as the doctor would have laid her down on the slab. "Take her out of this accursed place, to fire and light and the things of the living. If she was to lie in this place and awaken she would die of the horror."

The creeping daylight was coming into the long room, dimming the smoking and flaring lights. Dr. Abrahams looked at Madden; Madden looked at him. The two were troubled. The shock of finding himself in the coach with the dead had been too much for the young man's nervous system.

"Well, well," said Dr. Abrahams. "If you will have it so. It is only up a flight of steps and along a passage to my room. Let Madden take her."

But Terence L'Estrange would not give her up. He carried her up the stone steps, along a bare, high corridor, into a cheerful firelit room, with books and pictures about it. A decanter and glasses stood on the table. An old dog lay on the rug in front of the fire and wagged a friendly tail as they came in.

There, at last, he consented to be relieved of his burden.

He stood by, watching with a dumb expectancy, while the doctor did many things, Madden holding him the light. For some minutes there was a tense silence in the room. Terence L'Estrange, standing by, waiting for what he felt would be his death-warrant if the judgement should prove adverse. For what joy could there be in a world where beauty died young and must lie in the cold grave? What spell had the girl laid upon him that he should feel like this for her sake? He was bewildered—he, who a few hours ago had not a care in the world, and now was prepared to lose all joy if the dead, whom he had not known in life, were indeed dead.

Dr. Abrahams straightened himself from his stooping position, and said, in a very strange voice:

"And if she were to be alive after all, how are we to account for the profaned grave?"

Terence L'Estrange's heart sprang up.

"If she lives," he said, "the hearts broken by her death will not know how to praise you."

"Yours will be the praise," the doctor said, looking at him with the same moody gaze, "since, but for your madness, she would have awakened among the dead, and died of fear or gone mad, discovering where she was. And now will you take a seat while Madden and I try to discover if there is any wisdom in your madness? Mind, I do not say she lives."

☙

It was Terence L'Estrange who carried to the bereaved house, lonely amid its woods, the tale of how the dead had come alive. It was he who led the father and mother to Grace Dieu Hospital, where their faces were the first to meet their daughter's eyes as she wakened to full consciousness.

To be sure there was no hue and cry about the violated grave, and the thing was hushed up, though there had to be some explanation as to how Sheila O'Connell came back from the grave. So much was said and so much left to the imagination to fill in, about the affair that there was soon a whole story agoing in which body-snatchers and Terence L'Estrange to the rescue took the principal part. But none ever associated the body-snatching with that distinguished surgeon and lover of his kind, Dr. Jeremy Abrahams, whose name is written in the annals of medicine for certain famous discoveries of the utmost value and importance to the human race.

Sheila's father and mother could not make enough of Terry, whom they looked upon as one who, under God, had given them back their one child. Seeing that his father's house was overflowing with sons, and very little provision for any of them, to say nothing of numerous lovely and portionless daughters, they were for making a son of Terry, which Maurice L'Estrange, being unpractical, would not hear of. He could not spare one of his seven sons. However, when it came about in the way of giving Maurice L'Estrange another daughter in the person of Sheila, it was a different matter. So all ended as happily as possible, and Terence L'Estrange and Mrs. Terence lived to see their great-grandchildren about them before they departed this life full of years and honour.

Miss Mary

At the mouth of the bay there was a treacherous reef upon which many a fine vessel had gone to pieces. The sands had encroached on the shore, were still encroaching: only at low-tide the hull of a long-wrecked vessel showed through them. At night, according to the country people, the drowned sailors came back and sat there, a still row in the moonlight.

Beyond the sand were the salt-marshes, beyond the salt-marshes a few unproductive fields, where the sea-pink and the sea-poppy grew among the sparse, dry grasses that would hardly pasture a goat. Beyond the fields was a belt of woodland, holding the bay within its curves. Beyond the woods was the Castle of Waring. The Warings of Waring were now represented by Miss Mary, and were likely to die out soon enough, since . . . when people spoke of Miss Mary they tapped their foreheads with a smile or a sigh, according to their natures.

There had been a male heir to the name within the memory of people still in the prime of life. A bad egg, said the people, shaking their heads over Mr. Algernon Waring; and it was no wonder the Squire had driven him from his house and shut the door against him forever.

It was about that time the trouble with Miss Mary began. Up to the time when Squire Waring had bidden Mr. Algernon begone and no longer sully the air of the house in which his girl breathed her innocent breath, Miss Mary had seemed pretty much like other people; a little more dreamy and delicate than most: but dreams and delicacy are not uncommon with girls, and the Squire had been used from his one child's babyhood to listen greedily to tales of how the delicate children made the strong men and women, and so on, until the tale was of the blooming matrons with children about their knees who had developed from girls like his own, white as thistledown, unsubstantial as moonlight.

There had been no very good blood between him and Mr. Algernon at any time. Indeed, Miss Mary had not known her cousin except for a few weeks before the scene in which the Squire drove him from the house. A foolish thing, said the wiseacres at the time, for him ever to have admitted Mr. Algernon, with the character he bore; and more than one humble household had cause, beyond any the Squire had, to curse the hour of his coming to Waring. These things were kept from Miss Mary's ears. No knowledge of evil sullied the mild brown of her eyes with the great irises like the eyes of a child. She had the figure of a sylph or a fawn, and a gliding footstep which made her shadowy in her white gown as she walked in the woods at evening. She was always fond of solitude and twilight. For a little while, during that visit of Mr. Algernon's, she was no more solitary. After he had gone, she went back to her old, quiet ways, lonelier than ever.

The Squire was not one to notice. He sat poring over his books day after day, and knew as little of the woods and the sea as he did of the world. He saw no change in his girl: she had always been quiet. The first to notice was Mrs. Susan, Miss Mary's maid, who had been her devoted nurse. After a time, she brought the story to Mrs. Maythorne, the housekeeper. Maythorne watched her young mistress nervously for a little while. Yes, there was no doubt of it; it was as that kind, fond fool of a woman had said. There was something strange about Miss Mary. Perhaps she was so near the borders of a twilight world that it took but a little shock to push her over altogether. The change was so gradual, so all but imperceptible, that the Squire lived and died without taking any notice of it. He was found dead, with his cold face on an open book, about three o'clock of a summer morning, some four years after Algernon Waring had been driven from the house. He died still hoping that his Mary would marry, and grow buxom in time, and give him grandchildren, so that the place should never come to Algernon.

The two faithful women kept the secret till it could be no longer kept. Those things happened a quarter of a century ago, and, to look at Miss Mary in a bad light, you might think not half-a-dozen years had gone over her head. In a good light, you saw, indeed, the little network of fine lines about the eyes, so incongruous with the great irises. In a good light, you saw that the eyes were wool-gathering. Perhaps you noticed that the fingers moved aimlessly and were never still. Time seemed to have forgotten her else. She had the sylph-like figure, the gliding footstep, still. Her soft pale-brown hair had hardly a silver line. At a little distance and in a dim light she was the girl of twenty-five years ago.

She did nothing strange, nothing to oblige people to notice her affliction. Visitors to the Castle fell away, unless it was the lawyer on legal business, the parson on spiritual, the physician on matters of health.

After the late Squire's death, search had been made for Algernon Waring, to whom, by right, the Castle of Waring now belonged. If he would come forward, he could dispossess his cousin Mary of the ghostly old barrack among the pine-woods, the unproductive fields, the overgrown park. Very little else there was to come to him. The old Squire had seen to that.

Perhaps it was not worth Mr. Algernon's while to come forward. Perhaps he was dead. Anyhow, none wished to see his dark, handsome, reckless face again. He had done enough mischief while he stayed.

The Death Spancel

Miss Mary's trouble had kept her innocent, innocent as a five-year-old child. Anything so white, so innocent, so gently, faintly smiling there never was that had knowledge of the wickedness and sorrow of the world.

Of the great staff of servants that had once been at Waring only a few, too old to make a new venture, or too attached, remained. Besides Mrs. Maythorne and Mrs. Susan, there was Lovekind the gardener, Waggett the butler, and a couple of elderly housemaids.

Even though no one came, the house went on in its old formal, stately way; the rooms occupied by Miss Mary, the gardens and terraces over which her window looked, had nothing different from old days, when there was the eye of a master over the place.

The good people would have scorned to cheat anything so innocent and so unsuspecting as Miss Mary.

So the terraces shone like green satin. The beds were full of scarlet, azure, and gold, as of old; the peacock screamed as he spread his fans in the sun; the gold-fish swam in a clear basin; the gardens sent up their hot wafts of fragrance, as though to-morrow or the next day the place might not be shut up, going to ruins for want of a master or a mistress.

Maythorne and Susan between them petted Miss Mary as much as any child was ever petted. To see Mrs. Susan as she laundered and "got up" the delicate white muslins and laces for her mistress, she might have been a mother over the dainty little garments of a child. Of evenings, she dressed her lady in some soft thing of white silk or fine woollen, with a string of pearls about her neck and a blue ribbon in her soft hair; and no one seemed to find it incongruous that a woman nearly half-way through her century should be so attired.

Miss Mary did not seem to remember the passage of the years. It was only lately that Mrs. Susan, dressing her mistress one evening when the summer sun yet lingered, saw a line of bewilderment between the delicate brows while Miss Mary stared at herself in the glass as she might at a stranger.

After that, the glass met with an accident and was put out of sight. Other glasses followed its example. The long mirrors in the drawing-rooms were swathed. Miss Mary did not seem to notice. She had forgotten that momentary scare, since it had not been repeated, as though it had never been.

She wandered about a good deal by herself—safely, for Waring land was all about her, and even the bay where the lost ship lay buried was caught like a half-moon into the arms of Waring woods. Sometimes she had Mrs. Susan's attendance. Sometimes she had not. If she did not choose to have it, she could refuse it with a sweet imperiousness which showed she had not forgotten how to be mistress.

She loved the woods, and would sit there for hours while the sun was high, doing nothing but dreaming. Sometimes the dreams were happy ones, and then she smiled; sometimes they were sad, and then the bewilderment of her face was a piteous thing to see for anyone who loved her.

Someone from outside catching a glimpse of her one day, had incautiously remarked to Mrs. Susan that Miss Mary would never make old bones.

The good woman turned on the gossip furiously, with almost hysterical anger. Why, what would ail Miss Mary that she should be going when there were so many old to go before her?

They thought of Miss Mary still as young. To the old servants she was a perpetual child in the house. It did not occur to them to think of what would happen to her if she remained when they fell off, one by one. Only it sometimes troubled Mr. Freke, the lawyer, who was kindly as well as shrewd, and kept the affairs of Waring straight. He spoke of it once to his old wife.

"It would be worse," he said, "than changing nurses for a year-old child who had known but one nurse and never any mother."

But more than the woods Miss Mary loved the bay—Deadman's Bay, the country people called it. Her wanderings always ended up there. Mrs. Susan had found her in the twilight more than once, sitting on the hull of the lost vessel where it projected a foot from the sands. Doubtless her sitting there had kept up the superstition of the country people, who were not likely to come to close quarters with anything sitting by night in that haunted place.

It was very hot August weather, and Miss Mary grew restless. Perhaps it was the heat, perhaps the full moon. She was always a little restless when the moon was at the full. But now, like a child in the heat, she would not eat; she could not sleep; she wandered about the house at nights. She grew whiter, more transparent. That speech of the gossip's returned to Mrs. Susan's mind and made her sweat with fear while she tried to lose it in her anger.

One night, when everyone was asleep, Miss Mary got up, dressed herself, and went out. There was a magnificent golden harvest-moon, inclining to orange in the haze of heat that smoked over the country. She made her way through the pine-woods, across the fields; over the salt-marshes, and came out midway in the bay where the wreck of the ship was. Then her heart gave one great spring in her breast, and fell, feebly fluttering like a bird that has been shot. But it was joy and not anguish. At last! She had not kept count of time, and, perhaps, the years counted to her as months. But, anyhow, time had dragged, and it had been dreary. Now, at last, he was waiting for her, sitting on the hull of the vessel as he had so often waited in the old heavenly days.

She ran to him over the sea-sands noiselessly. He was sitting with his chin on his breast and did not seem to hear her coming—a swarthy man, with, if daylight had been there to reveal it, the face of a soul that has looked on Heaven and found Hell. Daylight, too, would have shown the dark hair thickly sown with grey, the haggard temples, the dead-tiredness of the whole face. But the orange moon in its heat-haze was kinder.

"Algernon," said a voice by his shoulder.

It might have been Juliet's voice in Verona, so thrilled was it with young ardour, so nightingale-sweet.

The man started and then drew back. "Mary!" he said, huskily. The voice was changed from the voice she remembered.

If he could have seen it, a mist fell over the radiance of her face. Then it lightened again; some pleasant thought had come to her.

"Mary!" repeated the man, still drawing away from her. "Are you a ghost, Mary, or have the years stood still? They had not prepared me for this."

She seemed hardly to have heard him. That new thought was thrilling and lighting her face, making it more and more radiant.

"Ah!" she said, "I find you sitting in the dead men's place, where so often we sat together when we were both of this world. I think I knew all the time, Algernon, that you were dead, else you would never have left me without a word. And so you have come back from the dead to keep tryst with me once again. Oh, what love, Algernon, what faith!"

For an instant the man's chin sank lower on his breast. Then it lifted stealthily and he looked at her with burning eyes.

"You might be out of Heaven, Mary," he said, "sent to lay a drop of water on a parched wretch's tongue. And yet . . . do you suppose he would be the better for that drop of water, knowing that once he might have slaked his thirst ocean-deep, and that now he must go parched for ever?"

She came a step nearer, anxiety clouding her radiant face as it might a child's who finds something said too difficult to understand.

"I don't understand, Algernon," she said, gently. "You can never thirst."

For a moment his lips parted as though the tongue were swollen within them. Then he said, with a gentleness almost equal to hers—

"Of course not, Mary. I was thinking of a poor wretch . . . "

Her thoughts were not following him. He had an odd idea that the gold of the moon was in her garments like a light, reflected in the pearls at her throat, making quiet fires of happiness in the depths of her eyes.

"Shall I sit by you, Algernon?" she asked. "You know I am not afraid of the dead. How often I came here to meet you in the old days, and many a time since! There never was anyone here. Perhaps I frightened them away. I have been here so often. How long is it since you left me, Algernon? I have forgotten."

The muslin of her gown brushed him and he moved away with an almost imperceptible movement.

"An eternity, Mary," he answered.

"I thought so too," she said. "But, of course, in months and weeks it has not really been long. I don't know when it was that it came to me you must be dead, since you had not sent me a word. After that, it was easy enough, except when—when I doubted. It was terrible while I thought you lived."

The man made an inarticulate sound of pity.

"And then Papa died," she went on, dreamily. "I used to think Papa was angry with you and had sent you away. But he was always good, to me, poor Papa! And then I used to think that there were terrible things said against you—things I could not speak of. Of course, it was not true."

Miss Mary

"Of course not, Mary," said the man, with a spasm of his face.

"And it was because you died you never came back? You loved me too well to leave me?"

"I never loved you so well as when I left you."

"And then you died, and you have come back to me. Will you come again, Algernon?"

"Perhaps . . . I may not be permitted, Mary. I came a long journey for this night. I shall have a long journey to go to where I am going. It is time I took that journey. And you, you must not wander at night, child. Promise me you will not come here at night."

"I am not afraid of the dead men, Algernon."

"I know. But promise me you will not come. You used always to obey me in the old days, Mary."

"I will do what you tell me, Algernon."

"And now you will go home: go home and sleep, and dream happy dreams, Mary."

"The time will not be long," she said, "now that I have seen you. I always knew that you loved me. But there were vexatious things that would return, things that were said and whispered. They can never come back again."

She stood looking at him an instant. Hitherto he had not so much as touched a fold of her garments. Now he moved nearer, and his face darkened as though the blood had rushed to it.

"Give me one kiss, Mary," he pleaded, "for the sake of old times, to serve me for that long, long journey, for the eternity in which I shall not kiss you again."

For a moment she was light as a snowflake in his arms. For a moment his lips were on hers.

"Your lips are not cold," she murmured. "They burn like fire."

"And yours are like the dews," he answered. "And now, run home, child. Your hair is wet with the sea-fog. See how it has covered the moon! And, remember, you are to come here no more. Dream happy dreams, my dear."

She went with a hanging head, her old habit of obedience making her go while she longed to stay. When she had gone a little way she looked back. The sea-fog had rolled in and hidden all the bay. But on the higher ground the moon was still shining.

Its light went with her all the way home. It flooded the silent house as she went up the stairs. Once, as she passed a muffled mirror, she smiled to herself, catching a shimmer as of silver in its depths, and remembering that once she had had a vision in a mirror of how she would look when she grew old.

The moonlight was on her face while she slept. Perhaps it was baleful, as they say the moon is. Anyhow, when Mrs. Susan came to the bedside in the morning, she cried out at the change in Miss Mary's face. Her age had found her out. Though the lips smiled and smiled, this was not the Miss Mary of yesterday.

But it was only that, in the night, the child's soul had escaped and left the body to the burden of its years. Miss Mary's heart had broken for joy.

The Ghost

Since you I loved are lost
    And all my hopes are vain,
Then come to me, a lonely ghost,
    Out of the night and rain.

O come to me a ghost
    And sit beside my fire,
I shall not fear you loved and lost
    And still my heart's desire.

O come to me again
    When stars are bright and keen,
O come and tap on the window-pane
    And I will let you in.

Eagerly will I come
    And set the window wide;
And bid you welcome to your home
    And to your own fireside.

O come, beloved ghost,
    When stars lean on the hill:
And I will warm you from the frost
    And from the night-wind chill.

The Death Spancel

You shall forget the grave,
    And I forget to weep:
Since the old comfort we shall have
    To lull us into sleep.

Fear! Is it fear of you,
    And on my breast your head?
I shall but fear the dawning new,
    And the cocks both white and red.

A Sentence of Death

She had known the Manor House from childhood with its one tender ghost—the ghost of a little child dead two hundred years ago, so gentle that none need fear it. It revealed itself to none, but one heard it of nights pattering up and down the attics overhead, where the line of windows were bricked up because of the long-vanished window tax; and, to be sure, who could the little ghost-child be but Mary Winthrop, *aetat* four years, whose epitaph in the church recorded that she was

All Beauty's essence, Wit's epitome

—at four years old!

But this was a sound unknown during the many quiet nights she had slept at the Manor House, unfrightened by Mary Winthrop's ghost. She heard the wheels turn in at the gateway, the wrought-iron gates of which were the pride of the country. Oddly enough she had not heard the gates clang though her windows were open, and it was a sound she always heard when a carriage entered.

She went to the window and looked out. The night was lit by a full moon. Everything was plain as day. Between the great elm trees outside the red-brick walls that bounded the Manor House grounds on this side she could see the wide stretch of common, and the church, all the gravestones shining whitely in the light.

A heavy, lumbering carriage had come through the gates, past the lodge, the occupants of which were all abed hours ago. It emerged from the deep shadow cast by the elms. There was something ominous about its heavy shape, even at a distance. It had four black horses, coming at a walking pace.

In spite of herself, Muriel Desborough uttered a faint shriek. Why, it was a hearse! The four black horses, with black trappings, the plumed carriage, the driver with his funeral garments. What brought such ill-omened things to Littlewood Manor House in the dead waste and middle of the night?

Muriel had only arrived in time for dinner. She had had very little opportunity for a talk with Lady Mary, the kind old lady who had made the Manor House a second home to Muriel since her father, the rector of Littlewood, had died. Muriel had always come and gone as she would at the Manor House; and some day she was likely to reign there in Lady Mary's stead, since Stephen Arden, Lady Mary's grandson and heir, was her lover.

Her lover had engrossed her; and she had had no time to talk to her dear old friend, who was the mother of all Littlewood and Greatwood-in-the-Marshes as well. Lady Mary took all her people's griefs and joys as her own. There ought to have been a shadow on her rosy old face, since someone, one of the many servants doubtless, must have been lying dead in the house at that moment. But Lady Mary had been as cheerful and smiling as usual. There had been music. Muriel had sung several songs. It was not like Lady Mary to have music and singing in the house when someone lay dead.

Muriel leant out of the window, watching with a fascinated terror the hearse approaching the house. She felt as though she wanted to run away and hide, but something held her feet where they were. She was possessed by a helpless terror. She wanted to shriek, to cry out for Stephen, her dear brave lover, who would die to save her from any suffering. Stephen was sleeping across the corridor only a few yards away. His name struggled in her throat for utterance, as though she were in the throes of a nightmare.

The hearse came slowly round the gravel-sweep in front of the house. She was conscious that her face, white in the moonlight, must be a conspicuous object, but she had no power to draw back.

The hearse stopped below her window and suddenly pulled up. The man who was driving stood up tall in the moonlight and looked into her face. He was pale, with long lantern jaws and small side whiskers. Conspicuous in the moonlight there showed on his cheek, and across the corner of one eye, a long deep scar, which looked like an old sword cut.

"Room for one, madame!" he said with a dreary jocularity, jerking his elbow backward in the direction of the hearse. She noticed that his accent was somewhat foreign.

At last she broke the spell of her terror. She wanted to wake someone, to tell someone the horror of what she had seen; but the self-restraint which is one of the lessons of our civilisation would not let her alarm the house. She sprang into bed and covered up her head like a frightened child. She lay shivering and sobbing with terror till she passed imperceptibly into sleep. When she awoke the broad daylight was in the room.

She had no doubt at all of what she had seen; and now in the broad daylight, with the birds all singing and the world refreshed by the dews, in this morning world it was hard to realise the terror of the night before. To be sure it had been ghastly; and the man had been insolent, doubtless taking her for a frightened maidservant, hanging out the window with a morbid curiosity.

After breakfast she walked with her lover in the garden. They had noticed at breakfast-time that she was pale, and had set it to the account of the London gaieties. She had been spending June with Stephen's sister, who was a very fashionable person and had had engagements for herself and Muriel day after day, night after night.

She had almost spoken then of what she had seen in the night; but something, she did not know what, had made her keep silence.

Now she told it all to Stephen Arden; and, being in a secluded alley, between a hedge of privet and one of sweet-briar, he had taken her in his arms and talked lover-talk to her which brought the roses to her cheeks.

"Soon I shall be always with you," he said. "And you will lose your fears in my arms. I am wild for September, aren't you, Muriel? You should have given me a shorter day—you should, indeed, or you should not have made me so much in love with you."

"I suppose Lady Mary did not like to tell me there was someone dead in the house," she said, rubbing her cheek softly against his hand. "I hope it is no old friend, Stephen; I think I know nearly all the servants."

"There is no one dead, dear," he said. "You were dreaming. It was a nightmare, of course. I wish I might have come to you and comforted you."

"It was not a dream, Stephen," she said, looking up at him seriously. "I was wide awake, I was indeed. And I saw it all so plainly. Why, I should know that horrible man if I saw him again. You know last night was full moonlight. It was light as day."

"There is no one dead at all events, in the house, Muriel," he said. "And you know we haven't got a banshee or hearse or anything of that sort, only little Mary Winthrop for a family ghost."

"But I saw it, Stephen," she persisted. "Could it have come in here by mistake? I did not hear it go away indeed, but, then, I had covered my head with the bedclothes."

"Poor little woman! You dreamt it. Hearses with four black horses and a driver with a sword-cut scar on his cheek, do not go driving over the country at dead of night, making calls at houses where they aren't wanted. I shouldn't tell her ladyship, by the way, darling. It might startle her, and you know her heart is not very strong."

"No, indeed; I shall not tell her. I kept back the question which was on my lips at breakfast-time. I shall say nothing about it."

"Put it out of your mind, darling," he said, stroking back her hair. "It frets me to see you so pale. Promise me you will think nothing more of it."

She promised him, as though one could promise for one's secret thoughts; but, strive as she might, she could not altogether shut the memory out of her mind. It would come over her at her happiest moments like a dark shadow. There must have been some meaning in the vision and the speech that were only for her.

Life at the Manor House flowed by in its old delightful way. It ought to have been halcyon weather for Muriel Desborough, with her devoted young lover always by her side, and the days running out their golden sands so fast till her wedding-day should dawn.

But there was a cloud on her fair, tranquil beauty. She did not sleep at night. Night after night she lay awake, wondering if she should hear again the lumbering thing stop at the gates, and the wheels crunch on the gravel.

She took to starting nervously, and she grew thin. It seemed to herself that she was always listening for something. She was absent-minded, even when her lover's lips were at her ear. At times the pupils of her eyes were dilated with nervous terrors. She would listen to Stephen while he painted in more golden contours than ever were on any painter's palette, the exquisiteness of the days when they should be together.

They were going to the Riviera for the honeymoon. It was not to be very prolonged because of dear old Lady Mary, from whom neither wished to be absent for long. And, to be sure, there was no place so dear as the Manor House, where already they were preparing the Bride's Rooms, under the happy supervision of the bridegroom.

There were a thousand delights and a thousand businesses. There were many visits to town, where the trousseau was being got ready. There were invitations to be sent out for the wedding, presents to be acknowledged, many communications with bridesmaids. Altogether the days were crowded with the most delightful happenings.

And Muriel must be consulted on every detail of the decoration and plenishing of the Bride's rooms, that were going to be hers. Her young lover was always seizing her, and carrying her off to decide this or that detail of the rooms which, according to him, were to be the most beautiful rooms in the world.

Muriel went through it all like a woman in a dream. At the back of her mind she was quite certain that the joy was not to be for her. The thing she had seen was a portent. Some day, some hour, before that wonderful 8th of September, she would be dead.

There were times when she could have cried out against the sad futility of it all. Her heart, which was so heavily sorry for herself, had sorrow to spare for Stephen, who was so ardent, so tender, so patient with her in these days.

Stephen watched her with an anxious and loving gaze when she was not watching him. He had felt the change in her. She was lifeless in his arms now where before her ardour had answered his own. She could hardly feign interest in the preparations for the wedding. Often he felt her sad, foreboding gaze upon him. Poor Stephen! she thought with a passionate pity. Poor Stephen, who was looking forward to a wedding, and must have all the sorrow instead! Her heart was so broken for Stephen in those days that she had hardly leisure to be sorry for herself.

Once or twice he had asked her what was troubling her, and if she still thought of her dream. She had shaken her head. It was no dream, she knew, though her poor boy would go on thinking it so. To all his entreaties that she would tell him what ailed her, she was dumb. Time enough when the blow must fall. Poor Stephen! let him be happy as long as he could!

But Stephen was not happy. He was thoroughly alarmed about the listlessness which had come upon his bright Muriel. She had a way of looking at him as from an immeasurable distance. While all the buzz of preparation went on about her, he saw her in a lonely isolation away from it all and wondered that no one else saw it but himself.

His anxiety made him wise. He paid a visit to Sir Mark Trevor, a famous nerve specialist, who had been his father's friend and was still his grandmother's. Sir Mark had, of course, been bidden to the wedding—but that was yet some weeks away, and to Stephen Arden's eyes Muriel did not look as though she could bear the strain of the weeks.

He told Sir Mark what he knew and what he suspected as to the cause of his fiancée's illness. His own face was white and strained as he looked in the calm, reassuring eyes of the great physician.

"Sir Mark," he said; "if I can't get her to put that accursed dream out of her head, perhaps it may come true. You never saw any girl as changed as Muriel. What am I to do?"

"Drop all the preparations for the big wedding Lady Mary wished for. Get a special licence, and marry Miss Denborough at once. Carry her off to Italy. That will put the thing out of her head, depend upon it. Poor little soul! It was a ghastly dream, to be sure. She will forget it."

"You really think so?"

"That is my prescription."

"I will do it. It will be a nine days' wonder, of course, and I shall have to satisfy Gran. I don't think Muriel will make any difficulty."

Sir Mark looked at him with a considering eye.

"Wait, my dear fellow," he said. "I can run down with you for a few hours. It will be easy for me to diagnose intense nervous strain after seeing Miss Desborough. I will tell my old friend that all the fuss must be avoided; that you must be married quietly at once and carry off the bride for complete change and rest. I'm sorry for you, my boy, I really am. I thought Miss Desborough one of the least likely girls I have ever met to be affected in this way. But you will see that my prescription will set her right."

Muriel made no demur to an early marriage. It was better so. What was the use of a great trousseau, orange-blossoms, bridesmaids, and all the rest of it, to a woman whose death warrant had been signed and sealed? She was glad indeed if it might be that she and Stephen should have a little time together as husband and wife, that they should not be altogether cheated of happiness.

She had brightened so much, indeed, in the few days that elapsed before the wedding took place that Stephen hoped she was going to forget all about her dream; and Lady Mary was a little inclined to be annoyed with Sir Mark Trevor. Ardens had always been married in a way to suit the importance of the family; and the abandonment of the great wedding had been a disappointment to many people, gentle and simple. After all, it was surely an unnecessary fuss about Muriel. Muriel was looking nearly as well as ever.

"We shall make up, Gran, when we come back," Stephen Arden said. "You can have all the festivities your heart desires, then."

He glanced at Muriel with a smile which expected an answering smile; and his heart sank. She was looking at him with a sadness and a great compassion. He guessed at the thought in her mind. There would be no coming back for her.

Well, he must hope and trust. He cast off his own depression, which would come upon him at times, whispering in his ear that his marriage was an unhappy, ill-omened one. Muriel's belief in the apparition at times made him almost believe in it as well.

They were married; and for a week or ten days the bride seemed to forget. In his first triumphant happiness the bridegroom had no room in his thoughts for death and fear and sorrow.

But slowly, after that first delirious happiness, there came back the brooding fear to the bride's eyes.

They were in a great hotel on the shores of the Mediterranean. It was wonderful weather. All day the blue sea and the blue sky out-stared each other, and the golden sun hung between them. The air was sweet with roses and violets. The place was full of well-dressed people, with the cheerful, smiling faces. There was nothing to whisper of death in the delightful gaiety of everything.

"It is too crowded for us, dear," Stephen said to Muriel, as they leant over the balcony of their room on the evening of their arrival. "We might have gone to Italy, instead. Why not Como? I know a quiet place there amid flowers, by the shores of the lake. Shall we go on there?"

The shadow fell on her eyes. Como or Monte Carlo, it was all the same. Wherever she was, the death would find her.

It might be an avalanche from the mountains, or the upsetting of a boat in the blue lake, or over yonder, in that wonderful sea, where the moon was leaving a long pale track in the water, and the silver of the stars was broken up in innumerable fragments. It might be—she had heard of someone who had been killed by the insecure railing of a balcony on which he leant giving way. She started back from the balcony, and her face was very pale. It was hard to die when one was so exquisitely happy.

She answered her husband gently that she was quite ready to go on to Como, if he wished; but this place was very beautiful. She was untraveled, out of the ordinary, and she felt the full wonder and delight of the world's beauty, or would have felt it, if there had not been always the lurking horror in the background.

The dressing-bell pealed through the big hotel. They turned from the beautiful prospect and went in to dress. It was a somewhat lengthy process, for Mrs. Arden had willed to do without a maid on her honeymoon trip, and her husband, although a willing, was a somewhat clumsy assistant. Besides, there were interludes. If he would leave off what he was doing to kiss Muriel's neck or her arms, things, naturally, would be delayed.

They were late going downstairs. Their room was on the top floor of the hotel, and as they came down the corridor some ladies, with a frou-frou of their flounce, bustled into the lift.

"Better go down in the lift," Stephen Arden said to his wife, "and wait for me at the other end."

He called to the lift attendant to wait. The man stepped forward into the corridor in the full glare of the electric light.

"All right, madame," he said, showing his teeth, "just room for one."

He had a pale face, with small side whiskers. One side of his face was disfigured by a long, deep scar. He spoke English well, with a markedly foreign accent.

Muriel Arden sprang back into her husband's arms with a little shriek. The man looked at her in amazement.

"Madame is not coming?" he said interrogatively.

"Madame prefers to walk down," Stephen Arden replied.

The man touched his cap and stepped back into the lift. Then—something dreadful happened. With a rattle and a scream something went down, down into the pit far below.

The machinery of the lift had given way, and the lift, when they were able to enter it, in the cellars of the building, held only the dying and the dead. The conductor of the lift had been killed instantaneously.

So the vision, after all, had come as a warning, and not as a doom. Why or wherefore it should have been sent, who can tell? It was one of the inexplicable things. But Muriel Arden, reigning in dear Lady Mary's place at Littlewood Manor, surrounded by her beautiful children, crowned with the love of her husband and the devotion of her friends and dependents, will now and again tell some very intimate friend of the strange happening.

"Why it should have been sent to me, and not to the other poor souls," she says, "is the inexplicable thing. Why should it have been?"

And no one has ever been able to suggest a satisfactory answer to the question.

She keeps the story for her intimates. Most people, indeed, looking at Mrs. Arden in her beautiful matronhood, would find it difficult to believe that she lay once for weeks under sentence of death—or believed she did.

The Dead Coach

At night when sick folk wakeful lie,
I heard the dead coach passing by,
And heard it passing wild and fleet,
And knew my time was come not yet.

Click-clack, click-clack, the hoofs went past,
Who takes the dead coach travels fast,
On and away through the wild night,
The dead must rest ere morning light.

If one might follow on its track
The coach and horses, midnight black,
Within should sit a shape of doom
That beckons one and all to come.

God pity them to-night who wait
To hear the dead coach at their gate,
And him who hears, though sense be dim,
The mournful dead coach stop for him.

He shall go down with a still face,
And mount the steps and take his place,
The door be shut, the order said!
How fast the pace is with the dead!

The Dead Coach

Click-clack, click-clack, the hour is chill,
The dead coach climbs the distant hill.
Now, God, the Father of us all,
Wipe Thou the widow's tears that fall!

The Body Snatching

Now that I was fallen so low was in some measure the fault of my hard fate, though I would not excuse myself. In the days of the late troubles my thoughts went as high as a star; but when those starry ones we followed had had their setting on the scaffold and in the grave, and for my part I lay in Newgate cells utterly forgotten, these things certainly made me mad. Four years of it I had, and never looked to see the daylight, except through bars, again. The despair and the dullness of my solitude had grown on my soul as the rust over a fine blade. I had come to making friends of the rats who came up to me from the sewers and the river, and tamed them so that they would sit to my foul food with me, and behave as prettily as a kitten or a dog. And God knows their companionship was the one thing that kept my soul from leaping stark naked into the abyss of madness. I owe them so much; and I have never since speared a rat, as once I could do carelessly enough, and often I have intervened to save them from others who had not my debt.

Then one day at the end of four years I was hauled from my cell to the blessed light of day, a suit of new clothes was hastily thrust upon me, I having been washed and shaved, and, escorted by warders, I was carried in a hackney coach to the Castle of Dublin.

I remember that, as I trod the velvety floors between the marble statuary and the paintings up the stairs that led to His Excellency's apartments—how well I knew it in the old days!—I caught sight of one coming to meet me who seemed strangely sad and distraught in this fine place.

The face seemed oddly familiar, and while I wondered to myself what had so soured his face and whitened his hair—for he was young—with a sudden pang I recognised myself in the great mirror at the end of the corridor. No wonder I had not recognised him who Eleonora Foster had loved, who was the gayest of the gays in the old days before the troubles had broken the country's heart.

I was yet quivering from the pang of recognition when I entered the room, which had only one occupant.

A tall, young, golden-haired man, dressed in plum colour, with a ribbon across his breast and a jewelled garter about the knee, stood with his back to the fire and watched my entry.

I confess I saw him but dimly. 'Twas a twilight world for me after that long sojourn in the darkness of my cell, albeit the glare was whiter than the whitest day.

Then I heard him command my escort to withdraw, and he and I were left alone.

The door was hardly closed upon them when he spoke, and he hardly spoke before he had one arm around my neck.

"Why, Jack! Jack de Renzy!" he cried. "I have been looking for you, man, high and low. 'Twas your own fault that you put aside your rank and carried a common fellow's name. 'Twas but a chance we found at last Sir John de Renzy in Patrick Houlihan. You might have died there. Ah, Jack, Jack, what have they done to you?"

Over all the years and the bitter, bitter changes I knew his voice. How often at Eton College by Windsor Town we had wandered through Berkshire meadows, that fond young arm flung round my neck as it now was! It was my own fault that I had lost sight of Humphrey. God knows I had heavier things to think upon than the old boyish love, and so his letters and messages went unanswered. And now to think that he should be here as the King's Viceroy, and I never to know!

So I was set at freedom, and had my friend's promise that my house and estate, made forfeit to the crown, should, if mortal means could do it, be restored to me. And equipped, by his love, with a fine horse and a purse of guineas, I rode out of Dublin gates on an embassy, the result of which should say whether it were better for me to be a free man and the Viceroy's friend or yet rotting in that dungeon.

I had no joy in my freedom, and though I rode fast on my way to Gowran Grange—to my shame be it said, with many a rowel point in the generous beast's side—I had no joy in the fierce riding, for the shadow lay over me of what was to come.

As I crossed Maryborough Heath I was stopped by Freney's men, and made at them so furiously with sword and pistol that they had finished me, if one of the party who had been with me in the late rising had not recognised me. Then they would have carried me to their captain and made much of me, but I was in no mind to tarry among those gallant robbers, and, seeing my desire to be gone, they sped me on my way with a blessing.

Three days and three nights it was before I came to Gowran Grange, and what I meditated to do there if I should find Sir Richard Foster and his son Anthony still playing the watchdog over Eleonora I did not consider. For certainly if the doors had been shut in my face six years ago they were not likely to be open today.

A rank, unwholesome, rotting August it was, and I had left Dublin in the grip of the smallpox. Nor did the country seem a whit more sound, for the whole air breathed of rotting vegetation, and I came to the cottages shut up and barred as though the plague had passed that way; and, indeed, it was true that it had scourged the villages.

The Body Snatching

The thin beasts stood in the fields and shivered. There were low mists curling off the hedgerows and creeping about the ground. I saw a fox slink about one of the empty houses. The birds came near me, as I paused, with the tameness of starvation. The winter was like to bury the summer's sick.

When I came to Gowran Grange at evenfall it stood empty. Why, I had known every minute of my ride since I had left Dublin, and the thing was no surprise to me. I turned away with an oath from the long ranges of black windows, with broken panes here and there. The house was like a dead body. And where now was I to seek Eleonora, who had been its life and light?

Well, people like Sir Richard Foster, his son and his niece were not likely to have slipped out of the world without leaving some trace.

At last, after much hunting, I came across an ancient crone, gathering sticks in the wood, who was so overcome by trepidation at my appearance that I had some difficulty in making her speak. She could tell me nothing but that they had gone away, that the house had been empty for more than two years.

"They are dead of the smallpox, most likely," she said, through her rotten, chattering teeth. "Everyone here is dead or blind. The famine will take the rest of us."

I put a guinea into her palm, and closed her fingers tightly upon it lest she should lose it. Then I rode back in the darkness slowly the way I had come.

I raged against myself now because I had not made inquiries concerning Sir Richard Foster. And now I had the long journey back before me and a tired beast, and hardly any place on the road where I could stable him and bed myself, for the troubles had swept across the country and its prosperity like a flight of locusts.

Alas! After all, I reached Dublin fast enough, and as I rode in by Bloody Bridge the tolling of the great bells of Christ Church and Patrick's shook the air.

"Is the King dead?" asked I, of a fellow who leaned on the parapet of the bridge and spat in the swirling flood.

"Nay," he said, "but the Lord Lieutenant is. This week back he has been sick of the smallpox, and is no more now than any Irish. I that spit in the river am more than he, seeing that I am alive to do it."

"I turned away sick with grief. It was too true; all the town had it, and I read it myself in the *Freeman's Journal* when I put up myself and my horse at the Bird in the Hand Inn in Mary's Abbey.

I saw him, by the intercession of one who knew that he loved me. And, Lord, it was a thing to sicken one of the world to see how that comeliness was marred. Yet I kissed him, careless of the danger to myself. His arm about my neck might have been the thing to hold me in the paths of virtue, even though Eleonora was lost forever. But now he was gone and my fortune with him, and my name even, for I retained that which I carried in prison. And presently, when I was sure that no seeking would bring Eleonora back to me, I railed upon that power which had taken him from youth and honour and love and even left me alive.

I went low enough, God knows, after that, only not too low for God to reach me. For a time I was with Freney, and again from time to time the companion of all the rogues and rapparees in the country. Yet, presently, because the solitary madness was upon me, I would ride alone and take my purses alone. I had still the horse my dear friend had given me, and a more leal friend I could not have. We took the ills of the world together, and he, a silky thing of Arabia, knew what it was to be stabled in the bogs and coated with mud down all his slender flanks; was often thankful enough for a handful of mouldy hay, drank brackish water, yet never looked less than love upon me.

But presently he had a ball in his flank from the guard of the King's mail, and, though we got away clear, I had to stable him for a month, or it might be two. Even I had my friends among the poor, and I knew a little farm in the mountains where they would cherish him for my sake.

So afoot I took the way to Dublin. I knew not what brought me there, nor what hope its dingy streets could hold for me. Yet I was drawn back. In all my wild living and through my evil courses, the face of Eleonora had not faded. Even yet I could not forbear looking up at house-windows, or in the faces of any I met, with a wild hope that was born only to be slain.

Christmas Eve awakened to a world of hoarfrost. It was welcome enough coming after a drenching season, to them who were not, like me, coated with the mud of the roads and wet through with sleeping out. But that day, as I walked through the fog of the frost, I felt my clothes freezing upon me till they rattled like a suit of armour. I had forgotten the days I was a gentleman. I could hardly keep myself alive for the cold. I should surely die of an ague, I thought, although hitherto I had a charmed life; and I should have so died, I think, if some charitable souls at a wayside inn had not warmed and fed me, albeit they looked at me askance, as though I were a bird of prey.

It was dark when I set out on the last stage of my journey; and it was nigh midnight when I trudged wearily under the wall of the old churchyard of Kilbride. It was pitchy dark then to see eyes unused like mine to seeing in the darkness, and even I could see but little.

Under the wall I found the trunk of a tree which invited me to rest. There was no hurry; Dublin had no hospitality for me that would not wait until the dawn; so I sat down, albeit with a shrewd expectation that I might wake up frozen if I should be careless enough to drop asleep.

The Death Spancel

I was, indeed, nodding when I heard the wheels of a cart approaching me through the darkness. I started suddenly awake, and, as it came nearer, I made out the figures of two men in a long, low country cart.

It came very softly. There was something of stealthiness, of fear, in the air of it at that hour of the night in such a place. Yet I started forward.

"I am frozen, good fellows!" I cried, "and can go no further! Will you, for God's sake"—how easily the old prayer started to my lips!—"take me somewhere where I shall have food and a fire?"

The light of a dark lantern flashed in my face and for a second was turned steadily upon me.

"It is the man we want," said one to the other, "since you had the confounded ill-luck to sprain your ankle. Where is the brandy bottle?"

In a second, a cup holding the pure spirit was held out to me. I drank it like water and felt returning the life in me go tingling through my veins.

"So you are sleeping out?" said the same voice. "You have an odd taste in a bed my friend, this night of all the year! If we had found you twelve hours hence you might have saved us some trouble!" He laughed, but even the laugh was below his breath, as his words had been.

"What would you do for a night by the fire and a golden guinea?" he went on.

"Anything," I answered, for the spirit was in my head, and, God knows, I was reckless enough before.

"You are the man for us," he replied. "We have a little job in yonder, and my friend is disabled for his part. Can you handle a spade?"

"For you," I replied, "seeing that your brandy has brought me to life. I won't pretend that I like the job, but I am ready."

"You speak like a gentleman," he said softly; and now the shadowy memory I had had of his voice took shape. Why, it was Brady—Ned Brady, who had been my comrade once, and of whom I had since heard as the leading surgeon at Madam Steeven's new hospital.

"I was one, once," I said, "but we need no gentility for what is before us. If the watchers are waiting for us, they may put an end to one worthless life and, for my part, I shall not blame them."

"Nor I," said Ned, "especially seeing that you have not the thirst of knowledge which leads men to do these things."

"There is too much talk," said I, "for the work that is in hand."

"Why, we are of the one mind," said he. "Come, another pull at the brandy-flask and then to work! But we have little to fear the watchers, since it is Christmas Eve."

He flung off his heavy countryman's coat, and he and I scaled the walls of the old churchyard, leaving the other behind with the cart.

The graveyard was overgrown to our knees. My eyes, that had learned to see like a cat's in the dark, looked upon a prairie of grey grass, silvered now with sharp frost and bristling like so many spear points. The night was lighter. As we stumbled over graves and with outstretched arms embraced buried headstones. Ned muttered that we would soon have the moon and no chance of escape if the watchers should surprise us.

"It will not be frozen hard," he went on, "since they buried her only today."

So it was the grave of a woman we were to desecrate. I had rather it were a man's. Yet I set my teeth to it, and the strong spirit helped to make me desperate.

The ground was hard enough. I had to take the pick to it, and the clink of it was enough to wake the sleepiest watchers, if any such were there. She, whoever it was, had none to keep that dreary watch for love of her poor tenement.

At last the coffin was uncovered. I was down in the grave fastening the ropes about it, when over our heads floated out the silver music of the city bells borne to us on the clear, frosty night. It might have been a singing of angels.

The bells still rung while we lifted the coffin. It was light enough for a young maid or child. Then Ned was kneeling beside it, prising it open with the tools he had brought. I turned away my head. I had no stomach for such work, and I would not look while he lifted the white thing from it and placed it within a sack. It was light and slender, and he needed no help. Such a pity for it and such a loathing for myself seized upon me that I had a sickness. I had thought I was harder.

I replaced the coffin and the clay hastily, Ned assisting me, while the helpless thing in the ignominy of the common sack lay out upon the grass.

We were soon done, and I took the tools to carry them. But, then, I knew not what madness came over me. Some desire to protect, to warm that poor body we had so wronged came upon me.

"Nay," said I, shoving Ned aside, "I will carry her."

I knew Ned of old and knew that nothing surprised him.

"All right, but quickly. Even yet we may be followed," and so saying he shouldered the pick and spade.

As for me, I lifted her with a quick shudder of delight. Then remembering that she was dead, my mood changed to tempestuous pity and despair. I held her against my heart. If my passion could have brought her to life, she would have lived. But, at least, they should not desecrate her. I made that oath to myself; if I had to kill the two, I would rescue that fair, piteous body, when I had looked upon the face.

The cart was heaped with honest sacks of potatoes. Of that I became aware by resting my hand upon one of them. I laid her first gently within the cart. Then I drew myself up, and, seating myself upon a sack again, I took her within my arms.

The Body Snatching

I heard Ned mutter something to the other that they had saddled themselves with a madman. But they let me be.

"When we come to the city gates," he said, "you will lay that among the other sacks."

"So that they go not over her," said I, for I still had the wit to perceive that I must not ride through the city clasping a sack of potatoes in my arms.

"There will be no need," said he, "though many a time I have made a seat of such a sack as you are carrying."

We reached the hospital without misadventure. The night was well chosen for such an enterprise as ours.

We entered through a narrow postern, which was immediately closed behind us, and, still carrying my burden, we crossed the dark gardens and into the lighted hall. A porter sat there in his great chair sleepily rubbing his eyes.

"Take this," said Ned to him, "and let this man have a seat by the fire for the night, and a meal to warm him."

"Nay," said I, "I will go with you."

"I thought you were going to give us trouble," said Ned. "It will be a case of a strait waistcoat, and Swift's. You have come to the wrong house."

Then he peered at me and a light broke over his face.

"Why," he said, "it is Jack de Renzy! I thought they had finished you in Newgate."

"I had not your discretion," said I, though it suited me best not to be so bitter. But I was mad at the moment, and Ned, like many another, had been a patriot in the good days.

But, though he winced, he spoke gently, taking my hand.

"Come with me," he said, "and bring her, if you will not leave her."

"Then I will go to my bed," said the other doctor. "I am in want of sleep."

"Then good-night," said Ned; "and it is a good night to me since I have found an old friend."

I followed him into a room fire-lit and lamp-lit. Through all my madness the warmth of it stole sweetly, caressingly, after the nipping night outside—or the dawn, rather, for now 'twas Christmas Day.

I hardly heard what Ned had said to me about food and drink and bed. I had laid her down on a couch and was gently withdrawing the sack from her body.

"She is past warming, Jack," he said with the utmost gentleness, and I know he thought my troubles had turned my brain.

"Nay," returned I, "for I felt her warm in my arms. No dead woman was ever so soft as she."

Then I uncovered her face and stood looking upon it with rapture. Why, I had known it from the moment I lifted her. The pure lids lay upon her cheeks. The hands were folded on her bosom. She was very pale. But, then, the frozen earth had gone near to killing her. She was as lovely as of old, and so I had found her.

"Is there a woman here," said I, "to take the grave-clothes from her and put on the garments of the living? Else, when she wakes, she may die of fear."

He had been watching me pityingly. Suddenly he stooped and lifted her hand. Something of surprise, of amazement, of fear, crossed his face. Then he passed his hand under the shroud, over her heart.

In a second he was at the door, screaming like a madman for the fellow who snored in the hall. The other doctor came, hot water was fetched, blankets were laid before the fire to receive her.

I went a little way off so as not to hinder them. I knew she lived, and that which they thought my madness was really but the madness from off my brain. O, how good God was that by the way of men's iniquity He led me to my felicity! It must needs have been because Eleonora prayed for me on earth and my mother in heaven.

So Eleonora lived, and Sir John de Renzy came back among his fellow men, and, as for the crimes, as well as the glorious madness of a common fellow known as Patrick Houlihan who was conspicuous in the late rebellion, they were all done with, or buried in the gentle breast of her who was so ready to forgive.

So we were married after she left the hospital, and she and I together faced her uncle, who had hidden her away in a vain endeavour to break her spirit, that is as bright and tempered as a Toledo blade. Together we demanded the restitution of her marriage, but alas, poor wretch, I came near to being as soft-hearted as my lady, and forgiving him. For his hunchback, Anthony, for whose sake he had sinned, was dead, and so all his wickedness had been for naught. Yet he repented not except after his fashion, and made an end of himself with his own pistols. For which may Heaven forgive him!

And afterward, since good things come not singly, I had a notification that, through the intercession of my dear dead friend, my estates were restored to me. I might have known it of him that he would put the matter in train without leaving it to any chances. And, since Mr. Pitt loved him, the thing was done.

So we are de Renzys of Castle de Renzy, and we have an heir to our name.

The Ghost

The air of the room chilled him to the bone, although a rosy fire leaped and sparkled in the grate, and outside the day was St. Luke's Summer.

"Ugh!" he said. "How cold it is, Cousin Juliet," and he shivered.

Juliet D'Arcy stood up by the marble mantelpiece. She was nearly the height of the low-ceiled room. She was a ripe, fair, golden-skinned girl, and her trailing gown of orange-tawny consorted well with her coiled fair plaits and the apricot bloom of her cheeks.

"I am never cold, Cousin Humphrey," she said. "But a good many people have made the same complaint about this room. It ought to be warm, for there is a fire here nearly all the year round. There are cellars underneath this part of the house, too, so it ought to be dry."

Except for the dank chill of the atmosphere the room was cheerful and pleasant, walled in old chintzes with a pattern of sprawling cabbage roses, carpeted in blue with a design of rose-wreaths. Every one of the chintz chairs and couches was comfortable; the feet sank in soft-piled rugs; there were all sorts of precious *bric-à-brac* about on shelves and in cabinets. It was lived in, too. There was an open book on a little table; another was heaped with books and magazines; an embroidery-frame was pushed into one corner; Lady D'Arcy's work-basket stood by her low chair.

"It is perhaps the autumn damp," Humphrey Aylmer replied.

The windows were not yet shuttered, although a shaded lamp had been lit. Between the silk hangings of the windows the park outside showed, heavy in mist. By day the prospect was a fair one. Miles and miles of coppice and undulating land; a herd of deer feeding, ready to go like the wind at the sound of a step; in middle distance the river, winding in and out glade and coppice; dim on the horizon a range of distant hills.

His eyes came back to his young cousin. She was pleasanter to look upon than the October afternoon landscape.

"Aunt Lucy still likes the Lodge?" he said.

"We are still in love with the Lodge," she answered. "It is such a dear little home-like house, so different from Grayfell among its melancholy moors. And this garden country is enchanting. You will see for yourself to-morrow. We have never regretted Grayfell. Then, this is so much nearer town, and there are pleasant neighbours."

There was the slightest hesitation as she concluded the speech. He looked at her kindly. How she had grown up, little Ju! She was quite a beauty. And in time Mary and Kate, her sisters, would be as handsome. He knew his aunt's wishes about him and Juliet. The girl was heartwhole, ready to be wooed and won. He had come with no unwilling mind to the wooing and winning, yet now that they were alone together he was in no haste to begin.

He had an idea that their being alone was his aunt's doing. It was Sunday afternoon, and she had found something she must do in her own room upstairs. The other two girls had gone out to visit a friend. A Sunday quiet was over the house. One imagined the servants reading their Bibles in their own premises. If a foot went along the corridor it went with a more subdued tread than of week-days. The Lodge, amid its gardens and park, felt the suspended animation of the great town like a heaviness.

"When I saw you last, Cousin Ju, you were only so high," he said, watching with lazy pleasure the lights and shadows of the fire on her face and her velvet gown.

"Before you went away?"

"Before I went away. I had no idea I should be gone for so long that you would have had time to grow completely out of my memory."

"I have grown, haven't I? Poor mamma!"—a smile played about the corners of her mouth. "It is hard on her to have three such enormous girls. You can't imagine what yards of material it takes to make us our dresses."

"I can only realise how excellent the result is in your case," he said.

The wooing and the winning were going to be very pleasant, he felt. She was as wholesome and delicious as a ripe fruit. Of almost too opulent beauty for her twenty years, she yet carried her youth in the swift lightness of her movements, in the shyness of her eyes. He liked to play with the shyness.

"You have been growing beautiful," he said, "while I have been growing old and ugly, burnt as black as a crow by the sun, tanned by the sea-wind. Do you know, Ju, that I am growing grey-haired?"

"Oh, no," she said, in a shocked way. "Why, you are not so much older than I. Nine years. When you were at Grayfell you were nineteen and I was ten, and I adored you. Quite young people are grey-haired nowadays. Old oh, no! Nor ugly! You are very far from being ugly, Cousin Humphrey."

He liked her vindication of him against his own half-jesting words.

"You were a dear little girl at ten," he said, and was pleased to see the shy perturbation of her face, which he thought to be for him.

She had looked up in a startled way at the window. Someone had passed it, coming along the terrace to the hall door. Aylmer, sitting with his back to the window, had not noticed the passing figure. There was a tinkle of the hall-door bell. The maid came in and announced "Mr. Hugh Young."

The owner of the name followed, a tall, fair, young giant, inconveniently big for the low room crowded with furniture. Juliet introduced the two men. Aylmer got up, remembering suddenly he had not had a pipe since lunch. He would smoke one on the lawn outside, while the light yet lingered.

He had two little rooms, just across the corridor, to his own use. They and the drawing-room were divided from the rest of the house by an arch; they were, in fact, the oldest portion of the house, and dated back some centuries.

His fire had been lit already in his bedroom, and had burnt up brightly; but there, too, the air struck coldly.

"It ought not to be cold," he said to himself. "I wonder, if by any chance, there is water in the cellars? The place smells like a grave."

He found his pipe and tobacco and went out. He had an idea that, if he stayed out long enough, Mr. Hugh Young might make his departure. While he walked up and down the maid-servant came and closed the outside shutters of the windows. The mist of the damp spread whiter and whiter across the park until the shapeless masses of the trees were swallowed up in it. He wished Mr. Hugh Young would go. What the deuce did the young puppy mean by coming in and monopolising Juliet? At the firelit hour, too, when he had been feeling so comfortable, so complaisant about that plan of Aunt Lucy's. It was time for him to give up roaming and settle down; quite time that he should give a mistress to King's Oak. And where could he find a girl sweeter, more wholesome, more stately, yet with a young charm, than his Cousin Juliet?

He began to fidget at length. Would the fellow never go? What was Aunt Lucy about? He wondered if Juliet often entertained Mr. Hugh Young *tête-à-tête*. To be sure, she had been left to entertain *him*. But that was different; they were cousins.

At last he shook out the ashes of his pipe violently on the green paling, and went back to the house. There was no-one in the drawing-room. It was in obscurity. Someone had taken away the lamp, and the fire had sunk to a little red glow.

A maid came along the corridor.

"If you please, sir," she said. "Miss Juliet took the lamp into the library for a minute. She will return directly."

He answered that it did not matter, and, sitting down to the piano, he began to play. That was something which had never deserted him, music and the solace of music. He was a born musician, and, with his hands on the keys, he lost consciousness of all that irked him or might irk him. He forgot himself, where he was, everything but the music.

As he played dreamily, passing from one thing to another, now improvising, again playing from a well-stored memory, he had suddenly the oddest sense of a presence in the room. There was the rustle of silk; something brushed against his shoulder; something lighter than thistle-down rested on his hair; touched his lips.

His hands fell from the keys. As the music ceased there was a sound like the winnowing of softest wings; something grey like the twilight went out by the open door; but, though it was shadowy, it had the eyes and the hair, the slender, sylph-like figure of a young girl.

He sprang to the door and caught sight of her, as he believed, entering the little suite of rooms that was his. He followed and found the first room in such dim firelight as the drawing-room had been. He fumbled for a candle and lit it. There was an arch between his bedroom and the other room, which was a dressing-room. He had hardly yet made acquaintance with it, since he had only come to the Lodge in time for lunch.

As he went in, holding the candle high above his head, he noticed the bitter chill in the fireless room. There was something cold and clinging about it. He looked round the room. It had little low windows, sunk deep in cavernous walls. The blinds were down over them. There was the same comfortable chintz-covered furniture which was all over the house. There was a big wardrobe. He opened the doors of it. There was within only emptiness. For the rest nothing could be more home-like than the aspect of the room. His bath was set ready for next morning, in the middle of the floor; the Lodge did not boast a bathroom. His dressing-gown was hung over the back of a chair. His portmanteau had been unstrapped and lay open, was apparently in process of unpacking.

He held the candle nearer to the pictures on the wall. They were old, dim oil-paintings. The sky and the olive-groves of Tuscany shone out of one. He went on to the next, a portrait.

Ah—he felt as if he had known the face always. It was suddenly as though he had left the normal, natural, living world behind, and stepped across the borders of the supernatural. He had been in many strange places of the world, had been in many perils and dangers, had known many excitements. Never had his heart beaten so violently before.

As he stared at the soft, pale, melancholy face of the portrait, he hardly wondered to hear a sigh at his ears. It was a little sigh, and for a moment there was the quiet breathing as of a young child somewhere close by him. The girl in the portrait wore a straight, short-waisted frock of white satin. She had pearls about her neck. There was a string of pearls in her hair. Her soft, childish arms were folded about a little lap-dog. There was something of the moony mystery of the pearls in the fair face, pale against a background of trees and darkness. The eyes were appealing.

As he replaced the picture the presence seemed to pass away from the room. The wind rose and sighed about the house. He was conscious of no supernatural fear, only of a great interest. Was it possible he had seen a ghost? And such a sweet one! Poor little lonely child, what was her history? She looked as though she needed comforting, tenderness. What an illusive, poetic little face it was!

He went back to the drawing-room, which once more was bright with fire and lamplight. Mr. Hugh Young and Juliet were alone in the room. When he came in the lad stood up to go, with an apology for so long a visit. He noticed that his cousin did not seek to detain her visitor. Looking at her, he had an odd idea that her ears listened finely, as though for a step on the stairs. Was it possible that Aunt Lucy's daughters were a little afraid of her? It struck him with a faint sympathetic amusement that Mr. Hugh Young was perhaps a person in disfavour with Lady D'Arcy.

After the youth had taken his departure Juliet came a little closer to him, and looked down at him with the fair and frank expression which had struck him at first as her greatest beauty. It was the more alluring because it was mixed now with something shy and mischievous.

"Cousin Humphrey," said she, "mamma, who has been asleep, I expect, all this afternoon—when she wants an afternoon nap she is always supposed to be reading or writing letters or turning out drawers; anything at all but having a nap—mamma would be very angry with me if she knew that I had been entertaining Mr. Hugh Young instead of you this afternoon."

"She need not know it so far as I am concerned, Cousin Ju," he answered, "and I congratulate you on your choice. He is a very fine specimen of young manhood."

At that she blushed rosily red.

"It has not come to a choice yet, Cousin Humphrey," she said.

"I should say it has on his side," he answered, enjoying the sight of her blushes. He forgot that a little while ago he had not felt so benevolent.

"He is a subaltern in a cavalry regiment," she said. "He only exists there by favour of his aunt. She means him to marry a rich girl. And I—you know that mamma's income dies with her; she has saved nothing—I ought to marry a rich man. Hugh talks of giving up the cavalry and going into an Indian regiment, where there would be the hard work of soldiering. He says that he feels he is where he is on false pretences. If he displeases Mrs. Molyneux—in his marriage, for instance—she will do nothing for him."

"It is a creditable attitude of mind for him. Still, tell him to wait a little, Cousin Ju. I am your nearest male relative, and I have more money than I know what to do with. Why should I not look after my young cousin?"

Her sisters came in, bringing a breath of the autumn evening with them. They were still immature, boyish, without the consciousness of sex. He said to himself that he was lucky to have such cousins. For the first time he felt a glow of pleasure in the possession of kindred.

Lady D'Arcy followed on her daughters' footsteps. The tea came in. Her Ladyship announced, with a little yawn behind her hand, that she had had a busy afternoon.

"Mr. Young called," said Juliet.

"Ah, I thought I heard a ring at the front door."

There was chagrin in the mother's voice. Aylmer said to himself that he was proud of Juliet. She might so easily have said nothing about the call. He had come at last to utter the question which had been on his lips for the last half-hour.

"There is a little portrait of a girl in my dressing-room, Aunt Lucy," he said. "It interests me. Do you know who it is?"

"Not at all, Humphrey. When I bought the Lodge I bought also a certain amount of its furniture. Those pictures were there when we came."

"Who were the previous owners of the Lodge?"

"A family named Warner. They had been at the Lodge from time immemorial. I gathered from something the house-agents said that the last representatives of the family were an old man and a child, grandfather and granddaughter. Even the sale of the Lodge meant little to them; there were so many claims to be satisfied. They were very poor, I believe."

He took occasion later on to ask Lady D'Arcy if there was any ghost-story in connection with the Lodge, telling her something of his experience.

"We have never seen anything," Lady D'Arcy replied. "Some of the servants said they saw or heard something. I put it down to the fancy of a hysterical housemaid. They are so easily alarmed. Such stories spread like wildfire. Already I find it difficult to keep servants here. The Lodge is so lonely, they say." She looked at him with an anxiety which made him laugh.

"I shall certainly not talk to the servants, Aunt Lucy," he said.

"Nor to the children?"

"I shall not be so ill-mannered as to pretend to a knowledge of this skeleton in the Lodge cupboard."

"Besides, you know, Humphrey, I believe it was an illusion of the firelight and the shadows. By the way, I heard your music in a dim way. It was enough to call up a ghost to hear it. What weird thing were you playing?"

He was relieved to find that she did not ask him where Juliet was at the time. She was so surprised at Humphrey's story that it put her daughter out of her head.

"I should never have given you that room, my dear Humphrey," she said, apologetically, "if I had believed in such stories. Would you like to change and go upstairs? You can have Arthur's room if you like."

Arthur was the only son of the house, a naval lieutenant, and away with his ship. "Not for worlds, my dear aunt," Humphrey said, with an emphasis that surprised the lady. "I assure you I am not at all afraid of ghosts." He was conscious, indeed, of a desire to see the ghost again, the strength of which rather surprised himself.

He had not long to wait. She came to him between sleep and waking. She was in his dreams. From the dark background of his sleep her little face glimmered pale as ivory. He came to know that face as it was revealed to him, far more distinctly than her portrait had revealed it. The face was hardly beautiful, only young and soft and pale, with limpid eyes, and a haze of dreams upon it for its expression. She hovered over him, reminding him of a picture he had seen somewhere of the Angel Guardian; her hands seemed extended over him in a tender protection.

She came night after night. If she left a sleep unvisited he was conscious of a strange loneliness. As he played in the dark of afternoons and evenings she would come and sit by the piano. Music always seemed to bring her. He used to play to her, putting a new spirit and heart into the music. He used to wonder at the others that they did not seem to see her sitting there, partly retired into the shadows, her face and her dress gleaming like moonlight. But apparently the vision of her was only for him.

He stayed on week after week at the Lodge. Lady D'Arcy was well-pleased about it, that he, who had always led a life of strenuous activities, should be content to settle down through October and November at the Lodge, where there was not even shooting to be done. She knew that he had many invitations elsewhere. They rained upon him once people knew that he had returned home. But he accepted none of them; it was pleasant, he said, to the delighted woman, to be with his kin—the only kin he had. Why should he go further for pleasure?

There was some subtle change about Humphrey. He was absent-minded, and at times a little odd in his manner. Lady D'Arcy had caught his eyes with an expression of seeing something where for her there was an empty room. And that passion of his for music! Every afternoon he was at the piano. He was plainly not pleased if he had to be anywhere else. And the sounds he awoke from the piano, which was an old thing, were something new in the experience of Lady D'Arcy and her children. It was uncanny, as Juliet said. Juliet was on those terms with Humphrey that she could say what she would. The music he drew from the old piano was uncannily beautiful.

He was quite well aware of the madness of his own obsession, though for the time he delivered himself to it. There were intervals when even the music did not bring her, and those were times of an arid loneliness and desolation to him. To be sure, when he could tear himself away from the Lodge, he used to combat his own folly. And he was uneasily conscious all the time that his aunt misinterpreted his willingness to stay.

He had meant to have done something for the young lovers before this. He had gone so far as to become friends with Mrs. Molyneux, who liked an adventurous man, and smiled kindly on Humphrey Aylmer from the first. He meant to pursue the friendship, to bring it to the point when he might broach the matter of her nephew and his young cousin. Juliet looked to him as a sort of Providence. It touched him to find her frank, trustful regard upon him.

At last it came to him that he must do something. He could not go on letting the little ghost fill the central niche in his life with her cold, incorporeal presence.

He presented himself in the consulting room of a famous nerve specialist. They had met before, and had conceived a cordial liking for each other.

"Don't tell me that you are among the patients," Sir Richard said, glancing casually at the face, over which a subtle difference had come since their last meeting. "I should have said that you were the soundest man I knew."

"What do you think," Aylmer said, quietly, "of a man who is in love with a ghost?"

"That a pretty girl would be a thousand times better."

Aylmer unpacked his story, and the doctor listened with interest.

"I don't doubt your word any more than I should doubt my own," he said, when Aylmer had finished. "You don't strike me as a person given to hallucinations. A good many men would tell you that your liver was out of order, your eyes wrong, your nerves gone to pieces. I see no trace of any of these things; but—if you are really sure that it is a ghost and, not some minx playing tricks on you—I would advise you first to go away. Get rid of the associations of the house. Afterwards, find a young lady of flesh and blood to drive out this intangible mistress of yours. Don't go back. Be done with it now this minute. I assure you that, if you allow the thing to go on, it will ultimately affect your mind. It is unwholesome, unnatural."

"Thank you," Aylmer said, with a wintry smile. "You have said precisely what I have been saying to myself. I believe it is very sound advice."

When he had left Harley Street he got down into Oxford Street and walked away westward. It was the dreariest hour of the day, the hour when vitality slackens and things seem not worthwhile. He walked as briskly as he could for the press of people. He wanted to be free of them, to be somewhere he could think his thoughts. The afternoon winter sun lit the sky with a cold splendour. It was full in his face as he went, dazzling in the absence of shade. All that great highway out of London was a golden path to the heart of the sun, which presently would drop below the horizon, giving way to a frosty night.

The light flooding his eyes and his brain became in time intolerable. Half-way down the Bayswater road he stopped in front of a red building of a curious shape. He had heard of the place before, but had never visited it. Why, here was the rest he sought, the quiet-thinking place far from the eyes of men.

He went into the building. Coming in from the aching light outside, he thought at first that he was alone. He sat down in a seat, and, leaning back, closed his eyes. It was an hour to sunset, at which time the building would be closed. All about him were pictures of the life of Our Lord on earth, comfortable, consoling pictures. He thought that the consolation was in the very air of the place. Blessed was she, he said to himself, whose thought it had been to set such a wayside inn for weary travellers.

Suddenly a little sigh broke on his ear, just such a tender, weary sigh as he had heard when that ghostly presence was near him. He started up, wide-eyed. Was it possible that she was going to follow him here, wherever he went?

No. He saw now that the person who had sighed was a young girl, who had fallen asleep in a seat a little way behind him. Her shabby hat had fallen off. Her face, drooping forward, supported, by her hand, was hidden by the pale hair which hung about her in a long, straight mass. She was sighing in her sleep. The attitude of her slender body was one of utter weariness.

He went towards her, knowing all the time what he should see. Why, the face was the face of the little ghost, but, thank God, a living, a breathing face. The ghost had prepared her the way. A sudden rush of great joy came over him. He had to control himself, or he would have taken the sleeping head to his breast.

She opened her eyes and gazed at him without much surprise. There was something almost of recognition in her gaze.

"My child," he said. He could hardly keep the pulsating passion out of his voice. "You had fallen asleep. You do not look well. Let me take you home."

There were great shadows under her eyes, painful hollows in her cheeks and about her temples. She tried to stand upright, but she reeled a little, and he understood.

"My God!" he cried; and the old caretaker of the place who had peeped in curiously was amazed at the anguish in his voice. "You are starving, starved. Come, I must get you some food at once."

She went with him like a child. He took her to the nearest place where food was to be found, and got her some soup. He watched her, while she ate it, with the eyes of a mother who sees her sick child feed, quite unconscious of the amazed faces about him, or the discrepancy between his own appearance and the shabby girl's.

She had only taken a few spoonsful when she stopped and looked at him as though she had suddenly remembered.

"My grandfather is ill in bed," she said, in a whisper. "He has had no food since yesterday. I had no money to buy him medicine. I was on my way to ask money from someone we used to know, when I felt ill and went into the chapel to rest."

"Finish your soup," he said, "and we will go to him. We will bring him all he wants. Neither you nor he will ever want for anything again."

He had no thought that he might seem rather mad to the girl, nor did she seem surprised. She looked at him with a passionate gratitude whilst she forced herself to eat some more of the soup. Her faithful brown eyes were the eyes of the ghost. He felt beside himself with joy because his ghost had become flesh and blood, because in the Chapel of Rest he had found his very heart's desire.

He was hardly surprised when she told him, as they drove to that wretched street in the purlieus of Oxford Street, where her grandfather lay dying of want in a garret under the roof, that her name was Lucia Warner.

"Everything went from us," she said, "in a long Chancery suit. My grandfather has been teaching the violin. He was wretchedly paid. Little by little even his tuitions fell off. And he is very old: I taught the piano; but when I became so shabby no one would admit me into their houses. Why do you care so much? Is it because God sent you and put it into your heart to pity us?"

"It is because God put it into my heart," he said.

Money can do much. The sick old man thought he was in Heaven when he woke up, after a journey in an ambulance, in a fresh, sweet room, amid a silence of green fields, broken only by the singing of birds. After all; since his illness was only heartbreak, with the addition of privation, he soon grew well, being happy and well-cared for, with the assurance of a peaceful old age before him. Being the dreamy visionary he was, it was hardly wonderful to him that Humphrey Aylmer should have fallen so suddenly and wildly in love with Lucia. It was easier to accept benefits from Lucia's husband; and the wooing was not long a-doing.

No one ever knew the circumstances in which Humphrey Aylmer had discovered Sir Michael Warner and his granddaughter. Everyone, save Lady D'Arcy, were agreed as to the exquisiteness of the bride, and the romantic and high-bred air of Sir Michael. And presently Lady D'Arcy was as much pleased with Hugh Young for a son-in-law as she could have been with Humphrey himself. To be sure, Mrs. Molyneux had behaved most handsomely to the young couple; and Juliet, thanks to her Cousin Humphrey, had not gone dowerless to her groom.

After a time, it was the most natural thing in the world that Lady D'Arcy, having two daughters to take about, should have grown tired of the Lodge and been ready to hand it over to those who, as she said, had the best right to it. Her little house in Kensington Gore pleased her a deal better.

The portrait of the ghost now hangs in the drawing-room at the Lodge, and is frequently taken for that of Mrs. Aylmer. The ghost never came again, although she might have been attracted by the wailing of old Sir Michael's violin in those ghost rooms which he had chosen for himself.

Ghosts are the last things one would ascribe to the Lodge nowadays. So cheerful a habitation, full of laughter and peace, of love, and the sound of children's voices could never harbour anything so sad as a ghost. Lady D'Arcy and her daughters, coming and going, notice that the unearthly chill has departed from the rooms that used to be called the ghost's.

"Depend on it," Lady D'Arcy says, "the house had stood so long empty that the damp had eaten its way in there. And now you have banished it, with fires and lights."

"Hearth-fires and home-lights," says Humphrey Aylmer, enigmatically. He has a theory that the little ghost grieved for those of her name who were in such sore straits, and now, in their well-being, is laid to rest.

The Spancel of Death

"Thank you, Sabina, you have done very nicely and your hands are so clever about one," said Lady Kathaleen Plunkett to her maid, turning upon her the gentlest eyes in the world, which were now filled with special kindness.

The long glass with its tall candles in sconces reflected the old room. The bedstead was like a catafalque and the furniture heavy and dark, but the mahogany was polished so that the wood fire in the grate sent leaping reflections of itself in every article. Outside the wind wailed, the old house was full of eerie sounds; but Sabina, otherwise Sib Doheny, had drawn every curtain over the windows and the room was cheerful enough in the firelight.

The glass reflected a charming picture. Lady Kathaleen was so slight and small that people often wondered how it was she was so dignified too. Her hair grew in a quaint way of its own. It was that pale hair which has as much silver as gold in it, and it went in successive ripples from the crown of her head down to her pure brow and around the little ears, where it hung loosely. It was short and fine, and silken, and very like the hair of a Florentine painter's angels. Her face was pure and pale, with innocent eyes, and a tender red mouth. She was dressed in white silk, short-waisted and quaint, cut in a straight line round her fair shoulders. Her grandmother's pearls were on her neck and about her gown. "Milk-white", an old ballad-writer would have called her.

The girl looking at her, half-defiantly, half-adoringly, was in curious contrast. She was so very vital. Her loose print gown could not disguise her splendid contours. Her dark skin was velvety as a peach, with brilliant colour, almost scarlet, on cheeks and lips. The eyes, under straight, sullen brows, had fires in their amber depths. As she stood she took unconsciously a pose of wonderful grace. This Eastern beauty in the wilds of Mayo was enough to take one's breath away.

Lady Kathaleen gathered together her mittens, her vinaigrette, and her lace handkerchief.

"And I am glad, Sabina, my dear," she said, with a sudden pretty flush, "you've made me pretty tonight, when my Harry comes to me after a long absence. And it's only when you get a sweetheart of your own you'll know how good it is to read in his eyes that he marvels at how fair you are."

Lady Kathaleen had an unusual affection for this maid of hers, or she would scarcely have been so confidential. Half-a-dozen years ago there was no lonelier creature in all the countryside than Sib Doheny—a lonely, fierce, haunted child. She lived with a witch, Mag Holon, in her hut in the woods. How she came there, and who was responsible for her, no one knew. She had always been beaten and ill-treated by the old woman from the time she could remember, and if she ventured from her covert, it was only to be set upon by the village boys with hooting and stone-throwing, which she responded to in her impotent way with strange curses and denunciations. The child certainly was a gipsy, wholly or in part, though none of the Coolacarrow folk guessed at such a solution of her yellow eyes and skin.

On some such scene of child-baiting Lady Kathaleen had come one day, driving her little pony-carriage, and was horrified through all her generous nature. The rabble scattered as if by magic before her, as she threw the little white reins to her groom, and darted impetuously to the miserable figure with its face hid for protection against a tree-trunk.

The gipsy child, furious and wretched, with her cheek bleeding from the blow of a stone, looked up at the fair little lady, like an image of gold or silver in the rich darkness of her velvet and furs.

"Oh you poor child," said the child who was only a month older, "how dare they! But they shall see how my father will punish them. See, I have wrung out my handkerchief in this cool stream, and I will wash away the blood from your poor cheek."

Lady Kathaleen was not satisfied till she had sent Jones, the groom, who bitterly disdained such service, back with the little girl to her wretched home in the woods. Sibby had never spoken at all during those astonishing ministrations, but curled up against the tree-trunk, had stared at her benefactress from under her tangled hair with dilated eyes.

The marquis' daughter was full of it when she went home, and had evidently taken to her protégée with that warmth a generous nature will give to one it has served. Lady Kathaleen was an only child, and a petted darling, and so the marchioness smiled indulgently when the marquis said, over the luncheon-table:

"Well, Kath, I suppose we must save this protégée of yours from the village boys, and from that exceedingly bad lot, old Mother Holon as well, eh? And put her to school, and make a Christian of her, and by and bye, when my little girl has grown to be a young lady she may serve as Lady Kathaleen's maid. Eh, Kath, is that what you would like?"

This fitted admirably, and so Sib Doheny was brought from Mother Holon and handed over to a school-master's wife in a neighbouring parish, to be licked into shape. She took quickly to her reading and writing, and soon became a fine scholar and grew a tall slip of a girl, with wide shoulders, and a promise of generous beauty, in a year or so. But a Christian, despite priest and schoolmaster, she did not grow to be. She was a pagan at heart, this full-bodied young creature, and though she was acquiescent enough, she scarcely heard the religious teaching that was given to her. She always was longing to be out in the wind and sun. In the gold corn she would lie for hours, when she could escape, her slim hands over her eyes, and her colour as vivid as her sisters', the poppies, which loved the sun as she did.

When she came back to Lady Kathaleen, there was no discouraging report of her, however. Sibby was so silent a creature that no one, and scarcely herself, knew that those lessons of reunification and humility had fluttered through her mind and left nothing behind.

She was certainly splendidly handsome, so much so that the good-natured marchioness doubted the wisdom of having such a girl in the house. However, Kathaleen was so fond of her, and then she was certainly well-behaved, and after six months or so, she had set no one by the ears as it had been prophesied she would set all the servants. She wanted none of the other maids' sweethearts, and after a trial of her haughtiness, the valet and the footman and all the rest, were quite content to return to their appreciative Janes and Marys.

Then she was very devoted to her young mistress, though even with her she never quite lost the sullen look which she had from her bitter upbringing, and she had nursed her very tenderly through the small-pox, bringing her through without a scar on her pretty skin, and running terrible risk of her own beauty.

So now one understands how Lady Kathaleen came to speak to her maid as she might to a dear girl-friend of her own rank.

Sibby followed her young mistress from the room and watched the dainty figure going down the long staircase, the wax lights on the walls making her hair shine like a silver cloud. At the last step Lady Kathaleen turned and kissed

The Death Spancel

her hand, with a pretty gesture; then she went through the folding doors into the great drawing-room.

Sabina turned to re-enter her lady's room, to put aside the gown she had just left off, and saw a gentleman coming down the corridor towards her. Sir Harry Massey, she knew this must be, as he had arrived half-an-hour ago. She drew aside to let him pass, holding back the red plush curtain that draped the arch of the staircase. He was a good-looking fellow, with the gait of a soldier, and a debonair brightness about his happy face and handsome curled head, which it was said had been found very irresistible by many fine ladies.

Sibby looked at him, not with the humility proper to her position, but straight out of her great eyes.

And he—heavens, he thought, what a woman! She was a goddess standing so, with her beautiful bronze head against the red curtain. Where on earth had she come from? They stared at each other for a moment—he with a kind of gasp—then he went swiftly down the stairs, and she dropped the curtain, and stood like one in a dream.

That night Lady Kathaleen's maid went up and down her mistress's room like a young panther. For the first time in her life her heart had awakened, with a madness and violence beyond expressing. She had looked once at this bonny young man, had seen the admiration in his eyes, had fallen madly, passionately, in love with him. That he was a gentleman of rank and fortune, and Lady Kathaleen's plighted husband she never remembered. She kept going over her memory for his face, hungrily, remembering with an exquisite exultation his startled look of eager approval of her beauty.

She brushed Lady Kathaleen's hair, and unrobed her, a little later, with no betrayal of the tumult going on within her. Her silence went unnoticed, for she was always silent, and her ladyship was in a dreamy mood tonight, smiling at her image in the glass, and with her eyes full of happy thoughts, such thoughts as one will not break the glamour of by speech.

Sabina never thought of her at all. She went through her duties quite mechanically, and received the usual gentle word of thanks. Somehow, Lady Kathaleen, herself, everything, seemed like the figures in a dream. The one overmastering reality for her was the face she had seen the first time tonight.

Dismissed, she went to her little room, not far from her young lady's but not to her usual sewing, over which she liked to dream an hour or two before going to bed. She took her peasant's cloak from the wall tonight and threw it round her, covering her head up in the outer cape. Then she ran quickly down the back staircase, unheard by those who were enjoying themselves in the servants' hall and out through a little door which would not be locked for a couple of hours probably, for Sir Harry's soldier servant, a fellow of prodigious jest, was regaling the downstairs folk with his quips, and they would scarcely break up until after midnight.

The wood was very dark this moonless night, and the wind full of omen, but Sib scarcely heeded, scarcely felt the ground over which her light feet carried her. She knew the place by heart, and there was no fear of her stumbling.

Mother Holon's hut was still alight, and the old woman crooning to herself in her basket chair by the bright embers. Her black cat was on her shoulder; her familiar the village folks believed it to be, and the stoutest urchin would not dare to pelt a stone at it. It was a poor place, and the girl shuddered looking around her at the cheap implements of witchcraft, the skull, the stuffed owl, with its glassy eyes over the door, the curious bottles; here she had suffered and been frightened in her lonely childhood.

The old woman received her with mock courtesy, with dreary mockery of her new estate. But her mood changed when the girl produced a golden coin carefully twisted up in a knot in her handkerchief.

"A love draught, my dear, is that what you want? Sure that's what all the girls want, and they only remember poor Mother Holon when no one else can help them. And for a gentleman! Well, who knows but he'll marry you. You're a fine, clean, handsome girl and sometimes I've heard tell gentlemen have married poor girls for love. Though not often, my dear—not often."

And the hideous old woman chuckled herself into a fit of coughing.

"Will you give me what I want," said the girl glowering, "and let me go? I want what will hold his heart and fancy to me, and away from them it's like to go after."

The old woman hobbled to her stores and produced a little phial containing a thick red liquor.

"You'll drop this oil on him, my dear, saying at the same time what I'm going to tell you." And she repeated a few words in Irish. "His heart will turn to you then from his fine ladies. Oh you'll remember poor Mother Holon, who's a poor old woman, hated by them fools in the village, and very poor, my dear. And if there's anything else she can do, you'll bring her another little bit of red gold just like this."

But the girl was gone in the darkness, closing the door behind her, and rushing away through the wood, with the phial safe in her bosom.

The next night Sib waited on the staircase to intercept Sir Harry again. As he came swinging along he caught sight of her, and smiled to himself. He was accustomed to his conquests in all classes of society—harmless conquests, to give him his due; and though he was quite honestly fond of his betrothed, he was not the man to deny himself a pleasant word with so handsome a girl as this. Last night he had been startled out of his usual careless gaiety at the apparition of such beauty; tonight he was his old self, and having learnt who the girl was, supposed her to be like most waiting-maids he had ever known of, and not over particular.

"Well, sweetheart," he said, as he came up; "two such happy meetings cannot be due to chance. I am a lucky fellow."

He leaned forward lightly to kiss her and felt suddenly a dash of something on his brow, which smarted a little; he heard a few wild words muttered between her teeth, and she was gone, flown like a deer, and he was standing dazed, looking at a drop like blood on his hand-kerchief, which he had wiped away from that tingling place on his forehead.

After that this young man's soul became a battleground. All of a sudden his pure love seemed to have gone far away from him; he seemed to see her across a waste of waters, as far from him as an angel in heaven might be to one in the outer darkness. Contrariwise, that witch-girl, whose lips he had only touched once, haunted him incessantly. I have said he was not a bad man; he was a good fellow, and under Lady Kathaleen's influence, he was becoming better every day. Now, the powers of good and evil fought furiously within him. He had had no experience in himself or another of this awakening of passion, of a passion that was curiously tinged with horror and repulsion. All that was good in him made a valiant stand against it, and he felt a yearning over unconscious Lady Kathaleen, which was poignant pain. It was love for one woman and passion for another striving incessantly to oust each other from his heart.

This went on for a week or ten days, which seemed to him an eternity. Things were not going at all to Sib's liking. He held himself away from her with an iron resolution, which only proved how strong Lady Kathaleen's saving influence had become. He went shooting all day, and only came in for

The Death Spancel

dinner quiet and tired. Lady Kathaleen had taken to waiting for him in the corridor now, and while he sat by her in the drawing-room, listening to her dear singing, his madness seemed to fall away from him.

Of course, he looked worn after even so short a spell. They were all anxious about him, and Lady Kathaleen was very tender and grieved when he told her about how his old wound had been troublesome. He would go to Dublin, he thought, in a day or two, to see a famous surgeon, who would soon put him to rights.

The crisis came quite suddenly. As he came home one evening through the wood, he found Sib in the path waiting for him. She was leaning against a great tree trunk with the fading sunset behind her, and her great eyes looking out of the shadows; she leaned there as if she were a little faint, as, indeed, she was with the violent throbbing of her heart. He would have turned aside if she had not stopped him with her hands outstretched, and a vehement rush of caressing Irish words, in her rich voice, low and as sweet as honey. As he looked at her, honour was forgotten. He caught her in his arms, he kissed her lips, and eyes and hair. He called her by every tender name he could think of.

As for Sib, she gave herself up to the dreamy delight of it, with no room for any other feeling. It grew almost dark while they were there, but time and the sun stood still for all they knew. The mountains were grey with mist, and they heard afar off the lowing of cows going home for the milking.

Suddenly there floated silvery on the air the sound of a bell: it was the Angelus, ringing; and, with the sound of it, Massey at Father Luke Halpin's little church, over at Clonakeely remembered God, and duty, and honour, and his love; and loosed the arms which were clinging round his neck like a Lilith's, and with a groan, turned away.

He looked very ill that night, and when all the house was

sleeping, except himself and the girl who bewitched him, and Lady Kathaleen was praying for him, he was walking up and down his room, half-mad with shame and trouble. The fruit of his life had suddenly withered to ashes. He said to himself that he was caught in as strange and shameful a coil as ever entrapped any man. This girl who blinded his senses, and set his every pulse throbbing—oh, no, he did not love her. Now, in his right mind, he *hated* her.

Meanwhile Sib was out on one of her unholy errands. She had before stolen the key of the little green door which let her in and out of the house, and as Coolacarrow was the most honest place on earth, old Conner, the butler, whose duty it was to lock up, never thought it worthwhile to mention the loss of the key.

To-night the girl was thrilling through and through with exultation. It was curious that she had never felt a pang of remorse for her ingratitude to the one friend she had ever known. But then she had no feeling of any kind except this undisciplined passion which swayed her wild heart.

She was bringing tonight what would prove a rare haul for Mag Holon. The old witch had worked on her with many promises, and now Sib was bringing her all her savings. In return she was to receive something which the old woman avowed would bind her lover to her forever.

An hour later, and if one had looked through the witch's window—as no Coolacarrow man, woman or child would ever dare to—they would have seen Sib on her knees by the fireplace, drawn as far as her position would permit away from the witch, who was holding something in her hands, something withered and brown and strange, rolled round and round, and tied here and there with coloured silk. It was like a thin string, some such thing as is used for making fiddle-strings, and as the old woman was unwinding it, it fell down her dirty skirt like a slender brown snake, eliciting a scream of nervous terror from the crouching girl.

"Look at it, Sib! Look at it, my girl!" shrieked the old woman, with a harsh peal of laughter. "Oh! It's well you may be afeared. There's few could look on the *booraugh washa*, the death spancel, without terror. Let him once have this fast on him, an' he'll wed none but you. The death spancel will bind him fast enough. It's brown now, and withered; but once it was white and soft, an' it took all my nerve, an' I was always a devil, to strip it off the pretty lady it belonged to. Eh? But the bonny lady I did this for gave me two hands full of gold for it."

Sib had heard vaguely of this awful form of necromancy; but now shuddered in every limb as she looked fearfully at its visible sign. The death spancel is an unbroken piece of skin, to be taken from head to heel of a dead person who must be kin to those it is to be used upon. This is done with ceremonies so awful that it would make this story too ghastly reading to detail them. Bound round the ankles of the man or woman who is to be the subject of the spell, and left there till the cockcrow, it is then to be worn always round the waist of the one who lays the spell, and he or she on whom the death spancel has been put is held so invisibly to the spell-worker that marriage with no other is possible.

It was nearly midnight when the unhappy girl left the witch's cottage with this terrible thing in her possession. It took all the unbridled strength of her passion to go through with the undertaking. It was a wild night, full of portents, with a rumble of thunder along the hills, and now and again a lurid streak of lightning on the horizon. Sib sped along like a hunted creature, not daring to look to one side or another for fear of the terrible things she must see.

The next night the spell was wrought. It was easily done, for Mag Holon had given her a powder to drop in the young man's drink, which plunged him in the deepest slumber. His dreams were terrible that night, as he remembered the next day, but he slept securely enough while the evil thing was bound upon him, and Sib watched outside his door, till, with the first windy breaking of dawn, the cocks crew, and then she took it and wound it round her own body.

Six years brought many changes. The wedding, which was to have meant such happiness, inexplicably never came off. It was a nine days' wonder. People shook their heads over Sir Harry Massey, and talked openly of the Massey madness. Just when everything appeared so full of promise, the young lover vanished—not in such a way as to allow anyone to think that he had been made away with—but he had gone to the ends of the earth it seemed, without explanation. He had been heard of in London and Paris, in wild company, and running amuck in wild exploits. Then he disappeared. One traveller had heard of him in America, another in savage parts of Africa. The old mansion was shut up and the estate managed by solicitors in Dublin. No word had come from the heir since that early spring morning when he had left his love's house without a word of farewell.

And Lady Kathaleen—how had it been with her? She had gone to death's door, poor child in that old trouble, which was so full of pain and shame. Then her father and mother had taken her abroad, to Egypt, to India, to new worlds of which she had only dreamed; and with the passage of years the intolerable burden became easier to bear. She never forgot, and never ceased to love the lover who had been so cruel. She, too, had accepted the old story of the Massey madness, and in that explanation had found cause for forgiveness.

As for Sib—well, her ill-fated passion had proven its own punishment. When she realised that the death spancel had but bound Harry Massey away from other women, and yet scarcely to her, she was like one who has given his soul for a great treasure, and has been cheated with flint for diamonds, and yellow clay for pure gold. Mag Holon had exhausted her magic in this last frightful spell and now her dreams and visions only told of a wanderer fleeing by land and sea, having taken his soul into his hands and fled with it. Sib had staked her everything on this one desperate throw, and lost. All the restlessness of her gipsy blood came into her. She stole out by night, wrapped in her peasant cloak. Some women, talking at the well, saw her face by the sickle young moon, and spoke to her; but she went on as silent as a shadow. And the veil of mystery had fallen over her then and hidden her from all who had known her name for six years.

However, when the six years were gone, Lady Kathaleen took a longing for home. The carriage passed through Coolacarrow one wild autumn noon and the villagers caught a glimpse of her—pure and fair as of old, though a little paler, smiling out at them, with a gleam of pallid sunset lighting up her pathetic smile.

Her father and mother had almost given up the hope that she would forget Massey now. She had been well loved; that wintry smile of hers which had brought a lump to her mother's throat to see, had won her more lovers than the most brilliant beauty could boast of. At least no man loved her without being the better for his love; and she sent none away with bitterness in his heart. She had gained, at last, great tranquillity after many prayers. She had come to believe her lover dead, and to be peaceful in thinking of him with God, as a woman might of her wandering son, gathered into a peaceful place where the rains will not rain, nor the winds blow, and "there are none sick".

Another wanderer had come home in the autumn—come home to die. Lady Kathaleen was only a day home when the messenger came. Sib Doheny was sick to death, lying in that ill-omened cabin in the woods, which was her only home to return to; deserted and half-unroofed. Mag Holon had died there, in circumstances so awful that the Coolacarrow folk would not refer to the death without the sign of the cross, and a terrified look over their shoulders.

Father Luke sent the message. The miserable woman had something on her mind which she would only reveal to Lady Kathaleen. He had been unable up to this to bring her any peace, her longing for this unburdening was so overpowering. But the confession once made, the tempest-tossed soul might find consolation of religion.

Lady Kathaleen went at once, leaving word for a messenger with food and wine and some necessary things to follow. The wood, which stretched down from the back of the church-yard and skirted the demesne wall was familiar ground. The marquis was out with his steward, seeing to many things; the marchioness was taking her afternoon sleep in her boudoir. Lady Kathaleen went alone with a great pity and concern in her face.

In the cottage it was almost dark. The fire was a handful of grey ashes. Mrs. Ryan, whom Father Luke had left in charge was gone on a long errand in the village. Till Lady Kathaleen's eyes got used to the darkness, she could see nothing, save two restless eyes—fierce and fever-stricken—looking up from the bed of straw in the corner. Presently the whole face grew out of the darkness. Oh, was this Sib? This mournful creature with blue lips fallen away from the teeth and the face, but for the eyes, of a living skeleton? Lady Kathaleen knelt down with a cold horror at her heart and a very agony of pity overmastering her.

"Don't touch me!" gasped a husky voice which had a ghostly echo of Sib's lovely richness of tone. "Don't touch me till I've told you everything. Oh, I'll tell, though she stood by me last night, grinning and threatening me. An'

The Death Spancel

when I've told you, you'll bury me in holy earth where she can't come?"

So, there in the darkness, the confession was made, and when Father Luke arrived and struck a light he was horrified to find Lady Kathaleen prone across the bed looking as nearly dead as the creature who lay with her last breath ebbing, convulsively clasping the silver crucifix which had been put into her hands. He gave conditional absolution here first, seeing that confession would never be made in this world. Then he got Lady Kathaleen to a part of the room where she should not see the dead girl when she recovered from her faint.

Later, she told the priest the terrible story she had listened to, and how Satan and all his fiends seemed to struggle with the dying girl to keep her story from being told. And only the crucifix, which Lady Kathaleen had taken from her neck, and held to the gasping lips, had given her the strength to speak.

They took the death spancel from, about Sib's waist, where it had been for many a year, and they said afterwards that when this was done a sudden peace had come upon the dead face. She was buried in holy ground, with the crucifix still between her hands; and the instrument of her spells which Father Luke was deeply horrified at the discovery of such Pagan sorcery among his people, took possession of and destroyed, burned to ash.

Lady Kathaleen was weak and nervous, after the shock of the terrible hour spent with the dying woman, but as she came back to her health there was a brightness to her face that had not been there for many a year.

And at the hour the death spancel was taken off Sib Doheny's body, a mad patient in a great asylum at the antipodes suddenly woke in his right mind. The case had puzzled the doctors exceedingly. It had been difficult to diagnose from the first, and here, out of a mad paroxysm, the fellow had awakened like a little child coming out of its rosy sleep. Worn and haggard he certainly was, but as sane-minded as possible. It was a great feather in the cap of the mad doctors, and all the more when it was discovered that he was a young baronet with £4,000 a year or so waiting for him overseas.

So a great Orient steamer is carrying him home to his sweetheart, whom so often in his delirium he had seen leaning over him with her divine pale face, like a saint in paradise, and her great compassionate eyes.

How happy they will be, whom God has not permitted the powers of hell to put asunder. They will be grave all their lives, as people may well be who have passed through such an experience; but they will be gravely happy, with an other-worldliness of thought and action scarcely impossible to us, who have only known the common experience of life. And so we will leave them.

The Dream House

To everyone who was sufficiently interested to have an opinion on the matter, with the exception of her husband's family, it appeared that Reggie Champneys had done as well for himself as he deserved when he married Miss Kitty De Vere, who danced at the Halls. Miss Kitty's dances were as modest as they were graceful; and she was a good little woman, quite uncorrupted by her surroundings, and with a full heart of charity towards all the world.

She would perhaps never have married Reggie if she could have guessed the immediate result; but she was too much in love with Reggie to consider anything but himself and his irresistible love-making during the very brief engagement that preceded their marriage. When she knew that the marriage had meant for Reggie being cut off with an angry shilling by his uncle, the Admiral, who had brought him up to be his heir, she felt a very guilty little woman indeed.

Reggie was a most unbusinesslike person, for it had never occurred to him that Kitty was making large sums at this time by her dancing. Unpractical fellow, he only wanted her to give up the dancing and retire into private life with him. He never even asked her the amount of her bank account, though he knew she had one; and as for her investments, the last thing he would have suspected was that Kitty was a business woman, and had made some very good investments indeed. He treated Kitty's earnings as though they were negligible, just enough to keep her in pin-money; and he took a serious view of the few hundreds a year which were left to him when he was cut out of his uncle's will, as being just enough to keep them going till he should get on at his work.

He was employed as a junior clerk in an insurance office, and even that was only by favour of an old friend of his family. He had a hundred and twenty pounds a year for sitting on an office stool, doing the work of a boy—for one doesn't learn the duties of clerkship all in a day.

It was a wretched job for Reggie Champneys, who loved a horse and a dog, and the green fields; who had hunted and shot and fished pretty well all the year round, till that evening when he had strolled into the Exotic and seen Kitty doing her Hummingbird Dance. He stuck to his stool with a dogged persistence which pleased the old friend of the family, who was a director of the insurance company, when it was reported to him by the heard clerk. Reggie really thought the hundred and twenty a year counted in the household expenses; and, to be sure, it did count in the masquerade of their first year of marriage.

For Kitty fell in with Reggie's simple ideas and beliefs. It was as good as a play to give up all her personal extravagances and to live with her dear boy in a tiny flat next the sky, so far above the noise of the streets that one hardly heard it, playing at being a poor clerk's wife. They had the flat entirely to themselves. Someone came in daily to do the housework. They were out for the greater part of the day, and had their meals in restaurants, except for the chafing-dish supper which they enjoyed so much after Kitty had come home from the Halls. So that there was not much housekeeping for Kitty to do. They seemed to live with wonderful cheapness, however, and Reggie was very proud of his wife's housekeeping qualities. He was putting by a good bit of the income; and he was increasingly anxious for Kitty to chuck public life and retire into a quiet domesticity.

A season ticket on one of the main lines and a tiny cottage with a garden was his ambition. Kitty used to smile to herself at the thoughts of it. She had her own plans.

Her contract with the Exotic was nearly up. She horrified her agent by telling him that she would not sign another, even at a bigger salary. There were reasons—a reason—why she should not dance much longer, which she kept to herself. Her visits to various house-agents was another secret.

She used to watch Reggie sometimes when he was unconscious of her scrutiny. He was getting the London pallor instead of the wholesome tan that had been his. The dull work, the sedentary life, the confined hours in a close, gaslight atmosphere, were telling on his good looks, but he had gained something to make up for the debonair freshness and gaiety he had lost. Something of strength, of endurance, had come into his face. His lips, which had smiled so gaily, were now more often compressed. She had wondered in the first days of the insurance office how long he would go through with it. Now she did not doubt that he would go through with it to the end, if he must.

She used to smile to herself when she thought of the bank balance and the investments. When she had found the place she was looking for and bought it, there would still be enough, with Reggie's few hundreds, to keep them going comfortably if neither were ever to do a stroke of work again. But she did not mean Reggie to have an idle life, nor did she think he would accept it at her hands. Reggie should farm, buy and sell cattle: he would be no amateur, for his uncle, the old Admiral, had been a famous farmer, and Reggie had learnt his business on the home farm at Champneys. He had talked of trying to get a job as a farm bailiff when his uncle had cast him off—if it had not been for Kitty's necessity for being in town. So the ideal place, when it was found, must have enough land for Reggie to farm. Perhaps when he had a place of his own he would give up sighing for Champneys, which would have been his had he not married her, and was now the property of a cousin.

He never openly sighed for anything he had relinquished for her sake; but he talked a deal of Champneys, describing the old place for her till she felt as though she knew it by heart.

It was not a smart show place, but just a comfortable, kindly old red-brick house, long and low, against a background of woods. He loved to talk about it, and she encouraged him. They would sit over their fire at night, he on the hearthrug resting against her knees, while she drew him on to talk of Champneys and the old days there. It was no wonder he dreamed of it and she dreamed of it.

One day she said to him that she believed she knew how the place looked just as well as he did.

He laughed at her, but she persisted.

"You would find it all quite different if you saw it," he said; and a cloud fell over his face, for she was little likely to see Champneys.

There was no love lost between Richard Burrill, present owner of Champneys, and himself. The old man had never liked Richard Burrill. If Reggie had not gone off so suddenly, before his anger had had time to cool, the Admiral would never have persisted in leaving Champneys to Richard Burrill. He had loved every mellowed brick of the place, every rood of earth, every tree, and he had brought up Reggie to love them. Was it likely he would have handed over Champneys to Richard Burrill, who had two or three other houses and could never care for it as he had taught Reggie to care for it?

The talks about Champneys generally ended up in a long silence, when Kitty would sit stroking her husband's hair and longing that she might give him back what he had forfeited for her sake. She had heard of many desirable things from house-agents, and had made several expeditions out of town to see them, rising in the morning hours when she was supposed to be resting, after her husband had gone off to the City. But she had been hard to please. Champneys had come between her and the bijou estates, the desirable small properties. If they had one thing Champneys possessed they had not another. If the house had oak wainscoting, the garden had not the yew hedges; if there were centuries-old mulberry trees, there was no pond in the garden full of silver carp.

She disappointed a good many hopeful house-agents before she realised that she was not getting a bit nearer to the realisation of her dream. It was Champneys she wanted for Reggie, and Champneys was shutting the door of all the eligible properties in her face. No wonder she dreamt of it all night, seeing it as she had seen it in pictures and photographs, going in at its old doors and finding her way about its rooms with a certainty as though she had known the place all her life.

Her contract had terminated, and she had made known to Reggie that she was resting—just resting. She would not tell him that she had given up the dancing till she could tell him other things; and Reggie, for his part, was very well content that she should rest, without being aware of any particular reason for it.

The time was turning to spring now, and the days were growing long. She spent whole days out of town seeing the places the house-agents sent her to. Her desk was stuffed full of "orders to view", which she kept carefully from Reggie's eyes. Reggie used to lament his enforced absence from her side now that she was free, and hoped the days did not hang too heavily on her hands. On Saturday afternoons and Sundays they made delightful expeditions out of town, travelling humbly in third-class carriages. Kitty never seemed to regret the motor-brougham of old days. They would lunch at an inn, have a good country tea at a cottage or farm-house, and come back to town in the evenings, their hands full of bluebells and primroses.

While they sat on a grassy bank by the roadside or in the woods, Reggie would wander on to talk of Champneys. Did a little stream trickle in the moss, there was just such another at Champneys; the long aisles of wood were like Champneys; a twisted chimney stack peering above the trees reminded him of Champneys; he would stand silent looking at some beautiful old house, stained with lichen and the weather, which had the colour of Champneys.

It became something of an obsession to the wife as well as to the husband.

"I dreamt of Champneys last night again," she would say. "I was in the Pink Room, with your great-aunt Maria's portrait above the chimney-piece. Shall I tell you just what it looked like? Shall I tell you the pattern of the curtains on the four-post bed? It was pink ivy-geranium on a green background. There was a glass on the dressing-table in the window shaped like a shell; and a door opened out of the room with two steps going up to it."

"I must have told you about it," he answered; and she assented, saying that she supposed he must have told her, and adding that she spent half her life at Champneys since she seemed to go there as soon as her eyes closed, and wander through its rooms and its gardens till she opened her eyes in the London flat.

She was looking a little pale and languid these days, and she noticed it one day with sudden alarm.

The spring had come in with soft south winds that brought a whiff of country air into the streets at night and in the early morning, when it could make itself felt above the fumes of the motor-buses. He spoke to her about going out of town for a while without him. There was money enough for that—she was such a wonderful little housekeeper.

She promised him she would think of it, adding that as she was in the country every night at Champneys she ought not to need a change. He took her little jest with a sigh, which she had not intended; and suggested, after a few minutes of absent-minded quiet, an inn which had entertained them on one of their walks. It was clean and comfortable, with a kindly landlady. Kitty would be happy there, and he would run down from Saturday to Monday.

That night in her dreams she walked in at the low door of Champneys, and felt that she was mistress of the place. Without a misgiving or a doubt she turned and walked under the arch draped with curtains, along the low, wide corridor, knowing exactly what she should see. She turned aside into the dim drawing-room, with its chairs and couches of red damask. Each side of the fireplace was an arched recess, the shelves loaded with china. Over the mantelpiece was the portrait of a child in a stiff frock of white satin. She knew the pictures on the walls, every one. There was a wonderful old Chinese cabinet by the door through which she entered. There were daffodils in clumps in tall blue vases. She moved amid it all as among her own familiar things.

She knew quite well the room that lay beyond; the bookroom with its groined ceiling, painted blue and gold and studded with stars. If she wanted a certain book she would have known exactly the place to go to in the shelves for it. The door opposite to the drawing-room led to the diningroom. She knew what she should find there, and which of the bedrooms upstairs was her own, and how one went the length of the corridor to come to the wide room of many windows which was the Champneys nursery.

Her vision of the place grew so clear and so detailed that she began to have a fear of it herself.

She lay awake one early morning going over the things she had seen while her husband slept. At half-past seven o'clock she heard the postman's knock and the fall of letters through the slit on to the floor of the passage. While Reggie turned on his side and asked what o'clock it was, she jumped out of bed and fetched the letters. She was usually content for him to do it when he got up to make her morning cup of tea. Reggie, who had been a young man about town last year, would let his wife lack for nothing of comfort that he could give her, although they were poor.

She heard him splashing in the bathroom while she read her letters. The sun lay on the floor of the room in a golden flood, and her canary was singing shrilly. She thought how beautiful it would be at Champneys now, crocuses and hyacinths in the formal beds; wall-flowers beginning to break into deep gold masses; the rhododendrons forming their great buds; the light, feathery green showing on everything.

Most of her letters were from house-agents. Only yesterday Reggie had remarked on the bigness of his wife's morning budget, and had accepted her reply that it was mainly circulars.

She read along without expecting anything very alluring, except on paper. She had grown used to the house-agents' ways. But—something held her attention—caught her breath. It was a letter from Messrs Lock & Flaunt—the usual stereotype letter, or almost—

> A delightful small residential property. Home farm attached, of about 80 acres, pasture and arable. Woodland, small park, at an unprecedentedly low price. Messrs. Lock & Flaunt have pleasure in enclosing an order to view.

But—the name of the place! It stared at her, jumped at her in the neat typewriting off the white page—Champneys, Alders Edge, Wiltshire.

She pushed the order to view out of sight under her pillow. She could hardly conceal her agitation, her impatience. How slow Reggie was! How deliberate over his shaving! He had his breakfast alone these mornings, having first brought her hers. How long it seemed till he came up to give her his farewell kiss!

But at last he was gone. She was alone, except for the servant, who had arrived at nine o'clock and was moving about the kitchen.

She jumped out of bed and made a hasty toilet, reminding herself all the time that it was no use being too early, since Messrs Lock & Flaunt's office would certainly not be opened before ten o'clock.

She had to wait nearly an hour before Mr. Humphrey Flaunt made his appearance. She sat in the office, turning over lists of houses, in a terror all the time lest she should let Champneys slip. As people began to come in on business she looked at them jealously. She wondered if anyone had had the order to view earlier than she had. She had just put the question to a weary and disillusioned-looking young man, when Mr. Flaunt arrived, with a rosy morning face, fresh from his residence in Surrey.

The good gentleman gasped at her precipitancy. Did Mrs. De Vere understand—Kitty kept her stage name for business purposes still—what she was proposing to do: to buy a house without seeing it, without discovering the reason for its cheapness?—for it was undoubtedly very cheap. Mr. Flaunt would not be doing his client justice if he did not discover the reason for the abnormal cheapness before she should close the business.

"As a matter of fact, we have seen and inspected the house," he said. "There is nothing wrong that we can discover. If you will leave the matter to us—"

"Please telegraph that I will take the house now, at once," said Kitty. "Or, if not, I will."

"My dear Mrs. De Vere—!"

Kitty had her way. The telegram was despatched, to be followed by a formal letter. After that a period of suspense for Kitty till the formalities were completed. During those days she gave Mr. Flaunt no rest. She was at the office every day. Never had a house-agent been so hustled and bustled.

In an unprecedentedly short time Kitty was owner of Champneys and all it contained, for the owners had been quite willing to sell the place as it stood, furniture and all. Mr. Flaunt understood that it had not been long in their possession, had been left to them unexpectedly by a distant relative, had been something of a white elephant to people who already had as many houses as they wished to keep.

"You've got the place dirt-cheap," he said, rubbing his hands. "And now that it is all settled I may tell you I've discovered the secret of the cheapness. There's a ghost—a ghost! Amusing, isn't it? What things people will believe! You don't mind the ghost, I expect?"

"I shall not be in the least afraid of a Champneys ghost," Kitty said, somewhat enigmatically to Mr. Flaunt's mind.

And then Kitty had to tell the great news to Reggie. Champneys was to be a birthday gift to him. His birthday was the 18th of April. Most luckily it coincided with the Easter holidays. Reggie was free for a few days.

Their breakfast was a little banquet—flowers and fruit on the table, fruit out of season, watery strawberries, green figs—which Reggie adored—all manner of dainties. He protested happily while he opened the legal-looking document that lay on his plate.

Of course, he thought he was mad, gone clean out of his seven senses, as he stared at the title-deeds of Champneys. He was so bewildered that Kitty had to keep hammering it into his head for quite a long time before he could believe it. Even during the breakfast—and he could eat, which was more than Kitty could—he would keep asking if it were true.

He had the sudden, delightful inspiration. "Let us go down there today."

"I was to see," said Kitty, looking at him shyly, "if everything is just as I dreamt it—if—if—the nursery is quite at the end of the corridor on the second floor. I wonder if they have kept it—as a nursery."

Reggie understood in a flash.

"You poor darling!" he said. "And so that was why you gave up your dancing."

There was a train fortunately—rather slow, but none the less certain. They got to Alders Edge somewhere about noonday. Everyone they met recognised Reggie, and seemed delighted to see him back again. One or two expressed a hope that he was come to stay. At the village inn they ordered lunch, having discovered that Mrs. Burrill was at Champneys, clearing out some of her property before the arrival of the new-comers.

"I wish 'twas you, sir," said Mrs. Merritt at the King's Arms, who had known Reggie from babyhood and was immensely pleased at seeing him again, especially with Mrs. Reggie.

"Supposing it was me!" said Reggie.

"You don't say so, sir!" cried Mrs. Merritt delightedly. "Dear me, I believe the Admiral *would* be pleased. They do say as he never meant to do it, only being took so sudden like, there it was. They say he walks, and that's why Mrs. Burrill couldn't abear the house."

After lunch they walked over the Champneys. As they came near the place Kitty had the strangest sense of having seen it all before. She could find her way blindfold through those woods. And the house—the house was the house of her dreams. She had known it all before—its beautiful mellow colour, the slight subsidence in the middle, as though the hand of Time had leant upon it very gently and pressed it down.

"I have been here before," she said, recognising this and that little detail that no picture could have given her.

While Reggie asked for Mrs. Burrill she peered beyond him into the hall, where the sun fell through coloured glass and diapered the dark floor and the old, faded rugs with brilliant colour. Not so had she seen it, but in moonlight, in dim light, in the grey dawn. And there was the arch through which she had passed. To find her dreams come so true puzzled and bewildered her.

She did not notice that the servant looked at her oddly. She gave her name, Mrs. De Vere. Reggie had agreed that there was no use in springing their identity on his cousin's wife, whom he did not know and was prepared to dislike.

They were shown into the drawing-room. A lady sat writing at an old-fashioned secretaire in the corner by the window. She stood up and advanced to meet them. Coming face to face with Kitty her expression changed: she looked startled, bewildered.

After all, she proved to be a much pleasanter person than Reggie Champneys had anticipated. She took them over the house, showing them everything. When they came downstairs to the dining-room, there was tea ready for them.

Under the influence of the kindly hospitality, Reggie Champneys became quite friendly.

"I think I ought to tell you," he said, "that we—I—am not unacquainted with this house."

"I thought so," Mrs. Burrill replied, looking oddly at Kitty; "and—Mrs. De Vere?"

"My wife has not been here before. I have—in the lifetime of the late owner, Admiral Champneys. I am—my name is—in fact"—bringing it out with a rush—"I am your husband's cousin, Reginald Champneys. My wife keeps her maiden name for professional purposes."

"I am very glad," Mrs. Burrill said, taking the matter very calmly, "that Champneys goes back to you. You have the best right to be here. But—don't think me mad—this house has been haunted by—"

"My uncle's ghost. So we were told in the village."

"No, not by the Admiral. The Admiral sleeps well, so far as I know: *but by your wife*. She has been here night after night. She has, in fact, obliged us to sell Champneys. Do you wonder that I looked queer when you came into the drawing-room, Mrs. Champneys? Perhaps, if I had known the ghost was a living woman, we would not have put Champneys on the house-agents' list."

"I have been here in my dreams over and over," said Kitty. "You see, my husband loved the place so much, missed it so dreadfully, I was always longing and longing to get it back for him. And he told me so much about it—"

"That you were able to project your astral body," Mrs. Burrill finished for her, "and to drive us out. Well, I am glad to be dispossessed by a Champneys. It is as it ought to be."

The Call

The unforgotten voices call at twilight,
In the grey dawning, in the quiet night hours;
Voices of mountains and of waters falling,
Voices of wood-doves in the tender valleys,
Voices of flowery meadows, golden cornfields:
Yea, all the lonely bog-lands have their voices.

Voices of church-bells over the green country,
Memories of home, of youth. O unforgotten!
When all the world's asleep the voices call me,
Come home, acushla, home! Why did you leave us?
The little voices hurt my heart to weeping,
There are small fingers plucking at my heart-strings.

Let me alone, be still, I will not hear you.
Why would I come to find the old places lonely?
They are all gone, the loving, the true-hearted;
Beautiful country of the dead, I come not:
How would I meet the cold eyes of the stranger?
All the nests of my heart are cold and empty.

I will not come for all your soft compelling,
Little fingers plucking me by the heart-strings,
In the grey dawning, in the quiet night-hours,
Because the dead, the darling dead, return not
And all the nests of my heart are cold and lonely.
They will not give me peace at dawn and twilight.

A Night in the Cathedral

The Dean's daughter, walking among the lilies in the Deanery garden, brushed some of the pollen of the lilies on to her white gown. Harry Wyndham, walking by her side, thought that she was like one of the lilies herself, with her creamy-white complexion, her golden head, the pure, firm chiselling of her features.

It was at a garden-party at the Deanery he had first seen her. He had been asked, as one of the officers of the garrison. She was walking with a grave, elderly man, a person of considerable distinction. He heard one lady say to another that Lord Castlecomer was too old for the Dean's daughter, to which the other replied that he was a great matrimonial *parti*, and that any woman's happiness would be safe with him. He was more concerned with statecraft than the fashionable vices, and despite the prick of jealousy Harry Wyndham had to acknowledge that he was handsome and noble, although no longer in his first youth.

All the sunlight of the garden seemed to Harry Wyndham to concentrate itself upon the golden head and the fair, pure face under the wide hat trimmed with roses. He rendered her some little service—stooping to remove a trailing briar from her skirt—and her eyes rested upon him. She smiled as she thanked him, and the smile made him her slave for life. He swore to himself that he had never seen anything to beautiful.

The Deanery sits in its garden, showing only one side to the street. The garden has a high red wall, on which fruit trees thrive. Within the garden it is hard to realise that outside there is a miserable slum, dirty, starving, nipped in winter, stifled in summer. Through the postern gate, when there was a garden-party at the Deanery, the slum faces looked, begrimed, pinched, hopeless sometimes, but not always debased. They brightened at the sight of the Dean's daughter. She gave the children fruit and flowers through the postern. Placing a spike of lilies in the hand of a pale child in its mother's arms she seemed to the young soldier like an angelic vision.

After that first meeting he went everywhere he had a chance of seeing her. He had the good luck to be invited to the Deanery itself, an old brown house, panelled throughout, which drowsed in the garden, all its windows open on a hot summer day, as though beyond were the hay-fields and the mountains, instead of the dreadful slums. He thought she had a look of sadness that day, as though the thought of the slum grieved her dear heart. She lacked, indeed, something of the gaiety proper to her youth, although she was so sweet. That day, as other days, Lord Castlecomer was by her side. His presence seemed to frighten away the young men. The old silver-haired Dean, who was a man of letters, was absently kind to Harry Wyndham. He came and stood by his side in the oriel of the drawing-room, which looked above the garden-wall to the cathedral. They could see the roof with its flying buttresses, the long line of windows beneath.

"It was here," said the Dean dreamily, "that my great predecessor wrote the *Travels*. In the room above this, which is occupied by my daughter, he lay ill in bed, looking across there to the cathedral where by torchlight they were digging the grave of the one creature he truly loved. What a memory! Most young women would be frightened of the room. Espérance loves it the better for its associations. You know our noble Gothic cathedral? There is not much in England to compare with it. A thousand pities it suffers from the damp. You know that it is below high-water mark to the river? When the river is high we are flooded. The floor should have a concrete bed to keep the water out. What can we do? We have no money."

The barracks where Harry Wyndham's regiment was quartered was but a stone's-throw away in the slum, under the walls of the old Norman castle. The other officers grumbled at the slums, at the airless, foetid place, the depressing surroundings. They escaped as often as they could. Not so Harry Wyndham. The ancient, squalid, picturesque streets were beautiful to him because her face sometimes lit them, because at any moment she might suddenly bloom upon his eyes, making the place paradise.

She was nearly always present at evensong in the cathedral. So much he had discovered; and since a day in which he did not see her was a day lost, he made a point of attending the evensong, sitting back in some shadowy place where he might see her come and go without her noticing him. It was easy to do that, for the vast cathedral was full of shadows. Except on Sundays the attendance was but a handful. Sitting in one of the unlit side aisles, the lights of the choir making a little coruscation in the far distance, he might well pass unobserved by the most observant; and she had a rapt and saintly air which looked neither to right nor left as she glided up the centre aisle.

Sometimes, when the lights had been extinguished, all by one or two, and the others gone away, she would stay for organ-practice. The organist, a lean young man, with visionary dark eyes, Wyndham suspected of being in love with Espérance. But then to the infatuated lover all the world must be in love with his mistress. Wyndham wondered at the folly of other men that they could see any other woman when Espérance was by.

He had carried his moonstruck passion from July to November, and in November, following a wet autumn, the slum was darker, more miserable, than ever. There was a sickness, too, which had broken out in the barracks as well as in the streets. The basements of the houses were flooded. A little unclean river, which flowed beneath the barracks, and was no more than a main sewer, although a few miles away it was a clear country stream, coming down from the mountains, overflowed into the basements of the houses, carrying sewage with it. The barracks was always more or less unhealthy. Now sickness became active. There was fever in the slums about. Life was a little more depressing than before.

The other officers were glad to escape as much as possible from their somewhat melancholy quarters. Not so Harry Wyndham. He was obsessed by the fair face and golden head of the Dean's daughter. He was anxious about her. Why didn't they take her away from the neighbourhood of the slum? Supposing she should take the fever? He knew that she went in and out like an angel, climbing the stairs of the foul rookeries, descending into their cellars, where people lived without light, without air. There were moments when he was wild with fear for her; when the tolling of the cathedral bell made his heart sink heavy as lead; when he was drawn to look at the long, low front of the Deanery, dreading, unreasonably, to find the blinds down, and known that the light of the world was eclipsed for him.

When they met she irradiated his day with a smile. He never tried to speak to her. Perhaps he was an unready lover. He had a curious content in seeing her at a little distance, in following behind her with a sense of protection. Not that it was needed. None would dare be rude to Espérance in the slum streets, where the people blessed the light of her face as she went by.

Day after day he made his pilgrimage of love at the hours when his fellows were to be found in clubs and drawing-rooms. The knowledge that he would find Espérance at the end glorified the wet streets, ill-paved, ill-lit, the low-fronted shops with their glimmering oil-lamps, the passers-by, frowsy and miserable. He would go with a light heart down the steps that descended to the cathedral from the street. He was always early so that he might see her come in. He had grown accustomed to the curious, damp, mouldering smell of the cathedral, which had become more pronounced of late. In the side aisle where he sat his feet were upon graves. The brass of the woman the great Dean had loved was under his feet. Above his head was the bust of the Dean, underneath it the strange bitter, terrible inscription by which he is fitly commemorated.

Wyndham had not been well. Indeed, he had lain on his bed in his quarters for an hour of an afternoon, with aches in his bones, wondering vaguely if he, too, was in for the low fever that hung about the old places, with the subterranean river flowing beneath them. He dozed, and the cathedral bell ringing for evensong awakened him. He went as he was, in his regimentals, his sword by his side, as he had come off parade, covering up his uniform with his heavy military cloak.

She was kneeling in the centre aisle as he came in and not in her usual place: she looked up at the clanking of his sword against the floor. Her eyes met his with a great kindness as he passed her by, going to the side aisle where he could watch her unobserved. It was kind of her to have knelt where he could see her at prayer, her quiet head bent in her hands, the great coil of her golden hair lit by the lights behind.

Evensong came to a close. The half-dozen ladies who had made the congregation tiptoed down the centre aisle and out into the wet streets. The clerics and the choristers departed by way of the vestry. Espérance, too, left her place and went up to where the organ was lit by a single light.

She was alone; the organist had gone. She began softly playing. Wyndham came nearer to her. He had a sudden sense

A Night in the Cathedral

of the vastness of the cathedral, its loneliness. Supposing any danger lurked for her there.

He came nearer, hiding in the shadow of a huge monument to a famous dead soldier that took up a great space in the side aisle. A tasteless thing, out of keeping, he had thought it, surrounded as it was by iron railings, the figure of the soldier raised upon a column. A graveyard had been its proper place.

He sat down in the shadow of the thing listening to the music. It seemed to him that she played for him. He resolved within himself that he would speak to her as she went out—walk with her to the Deanery. Who could tell but she might invite him within? He had a vision of her in a fire-lit room, the rosy glow of her bright head. Espérance! Espérance!

She was playing something that might have been a strain out of heaven. He leant forward, his elbows on his knees, his face in his hands. His head ached intolerably. There was a miasma of something near him. He felt faint.

Certainly the cathedral was not healthy. He remembered what the Dean had told him; the rising of the water in the subterranean river and the sewers. The dead were under his feet. He thought he would go and tell Espérance that she ought not to be there, inhaling one knew not what foul vapours. He tried to rise, but he dropped in his seat again, sick and faint. The music went on through the roaring of waters in his ears. Then there was a blank space.

He came to himself in a thick darkness. He was cold and faint, but the throbbing and pain had departed. There was something cold about his feet, rising higher and higher. Perhaps it was that which had awakened him.

He felt about him for matches and found none. To be sure, one did not smoke on parade. He looked up at the windows near him. They were stained glass, and gave no hint at all of the lighter sky outside. He remembered—to be sure, he must have dozed off, or been overcome by the foul smells, and Espérance had gone away, not knowing that he hid there in the shadow of the field-marshal's monument. He would have to stay in all night, he supposed. And in the dark!

He drew his feet up out of the wet on the floor, standing on the seat. Through the darkness he could see the field-marshal towering above him. He wondered what hour it was—a bore not to know.

Feeling his way by the ends of the seats he got to the door by which he had entered. It was locked. No chance that way. He turned about, with outstretched hands groping his way towards the vestry. The water was now swishing about his feet. It had begun with a little ooze. He had noticed without surprise earlier that the floor was damp. Now the water must be forcing its way through every nook and cranny. He was not afraid of the water. It was unpleasant, but he did not suppose that it would rise very high, not dangerously high at least. He supposed the vaults below were full, and the coffins floating about. He had heard that such things happened.

He had an inspiration. Supposing he could strike a light? He might be able to light one of the old-fashioned gas jets with which the cathedral still was lit. The organ—there were candles by the organ. He might find the matches. The matches would surely be somewhere about. To light the cathedral would surely shorten his imprisonment, if anyone were awake to see. He had no idea what hour it was. But there seemed a cessation of life in the busy, noisy streets outside.

The water was now flowing strongly about his feet. It was foul, but it brought also a sensation of freshness, like a wind blowing into the poisoned atmosphere.

As he groped his way up the central aisle he was suddenly aware that he was not alone of living things in the fast-rising flood. Something thudded against his legs, swimming strongly. A rat! Why, there was more than one. There was a whole shoal of them swimming like porpoises. How they squeaked and squealed! Suddenly one of them nipped him on the leg.

They were as thick as bees! He was at the organ now, and he drew himself beyond their reach on to the organist's stool while he felt for the matches. Incredible luck! He found them on a little ledge by the candle. He struck a light. There was a huge scurrying and squeaking.

Lifting the candle above his head he looked down at the rising flood, which by this time covered the floor to the depth of a couple of feet. The little light flashed about him, making the darkness of the great cathedral a thing to be felt. The floor below him was alive with struggling bodies and sharp, eager eyes. To be sure, the rats were being drowned in the sewers. They had found a way up. The place was alive with them.

Suddenly, with a great shock, he understood his peril. Myriads of ravenous eyes seemed directed upon him and his light. The sleek, wet backs were directing their way towards him. A rat leaped out of the mass and bit him. Ah, his leg was bleeding where one of the first-comers had nipped him! The rats were hungry!

For a second he stood in a sick terror, doing nothing. Then he remembered his sword, and slashed at the nearest rat.

The beast squeaked shrilly, and then—his comrades had torn him down and devoured him. Wyndham slashed again and again, still holding the candle erect. He must escape somehow, before they dragged him down and devoured him as they were devouring each other, down there in the darkness.

If he could but have reached the vestry, or the bell-tower! No chance of either. He would be torn to pieces and eaten long before he could cross that living floor.

Ah, the field-marshal's monument! It was still possible to reach it over the choir-stalls and the benches without going down into that inferno. It could climb the pillar and stand beside the field-marshal it would, at least, give him time. No chance of lightening up the gas jets, as he had hoped. If only the candle would hold out! Flashing it suddenly it seemed to have a momentary deterrent effect on the rats.

"One—need—not—die—in the dark!"

He heard the words as though someone had spoken them close by him, not himself. Horror seemed to have given him new strength. He clambered over the choir-stalls and the benches, the sleek heads lifted out of the water, leaping at him as he went on. Now and again he slashed at a rat that was climbing towards him, and saw it vanish with a squeak, pulled down by its fellows.

He reached the railings of the tomb. Thank heaven, they were fine floriated railings, the design of the lower portion small and delicate. It gave him time. He swarmed up the pillar, and dragged himself on to the platform at the top. On the great soldier's extended hand he set the candle. Then he looked down.

He was only just in time. The rats, baffled at first, were climbing the iron-work, dropping into the water, with one thud after another, where the widening of the railings allowed them to pass through. They were swarming about the base of the monument, struggling and squealing, as though they fought for the first possession of the man above them. They were climbing on each other's backs out of the water, coming nearer, nearer.

He set his back against the bronze cloak of the field-marshal. At least they could not attack him from his behind. He was going to sell his life dearly, but what was one man against a million rats?

A horrid memory floated though his brain of a woman who had fallen into the underground river, which had egress by trap-doors into the back yards of the slum, and had been carried away under the houses. Nor had anything of her come to light, though they had looked for her body at the point where the hidden river with all its sewage empties itself into the greater river that carried all out to sea. "Eaten by the rats," someone had said.

Eaten by the rats! Again he heard the words, as though someone else had spoken them. He had let his cloak fall. The rats swarmed over it, climbing upon each other. As far as he could see the floor of the cathedral was alive, a slimy mass that moved, moved. The slimy mass, else dull, was lit by myriads of eyes like points of lights.

He slashed at the nearest rats with his sword, and heard them squeal. But as fast as they went down, their fellows came on. He slashed, slashed till his arm ached with fatigue. What was the use? He was only staving off the inevitable end.

The water had ceased to rise. The tide must have turned, and was running out in the river. Perhaps, if only he could hold out, the rats might return to their lairs. But how long could he hold out? If he were to fall now—and a desperate fatigue had come upon him—they would make short work of him. A few clean-picked bones, that would be all. A vision floated into his mind of the Dean's daughter, pale and golden-haired, like a lily or an angel. What an end for the man who had dared to love her! To be eaten by the rats—alive, not mercifully dead.

For the end must come soon. The foremost of the rats, before he could cut him down, had nipped his hand, making it bleed. Why, he was bleeding from many points. There was a rat half-way up his leg. Slashing at it he made a deeper wound in his leg. The blood running down drew the hungry beasts upon him. He knew there was blood all about his feet—his own or the rats'. His hands were smeared with it. It was all over the sword; it was blunting the sword's keen edge. He wondered if there was enough edge left upon it to kill himself before he could be eaten piecemeal.

He paused for a second, trembling with exhaustion. He flung an arm about the neck of the field-marshal to save himself from falling forward. Something bit his head. The rats were coming up that way, from behind. One was clawing at his hair. They were taking him by surprise.

He remembered the *hari-kari* of the Japanese. *To fall upon his sword!* That might let his life out before the unspeakable horror of being eaten alive came upon him!

To fall upon his sword! Had someone spoken the words close to his ear? The rats had him now, climbing the statue from the back. One bit his ear. He turned about and attacked them with a fury that gave him new strength. But what use for one man to fight against myriads?

The water had sunk; was receding through the cracks of the floor with a rushing and bubbling noise. He was not aware of it. Making his last desperate fight he was quite unconscious of the door of the cathedral flung violently open—of light, the shouting of men's voices, the scurrying of rats to their holes, open once more. It was too much; it was over. He tried to turn the sword towards himself, but it dropped from his hand, slimy with blood; dropped with a ringing sound to the floor. He would have toppled down himself—on to the sharp spear-points of the railings—if he had not been caught in the arms of friends.

☙

He came to himself in a four-poster bed, hung with curtains of old chintz, the pattern of which was roses on a trellis. The room was brown and panelled. The fire was purring a little song on the hearth. There was the singing of a kettle in the room. The window was open. For once November breathed like May. The tiny song of a robin, full of hope and cheer, was not a stone's-throw off.

He was sore from head to foot and very weak. He had a feeling of having been in hell; but this was not hell. There was something in the atmosphere of the room, a shining, more like heaven. Ah! He began to remember.

A Night in the Cathedral

The kind, not very wise face of an elderly woman came to the side of the bed and looked down at him; then disappeared. He heard her voice calling outside the bedroom door:

"Mr. Dean, Mr. Dean, the gentleman's come to himself."

Then slow steps came up the stairs; and in another moment Dean Congreve's face was looking down at him. So he was in the Deanery. It was *her* atmosphere—that of the shining ones of heaven.

"My dear boy, I am so glad you are awake. You are quite all right after your terrible experience. There, don't think. We have to nurse you back to forgetfulness. My daughter will be so glad. It was so fortunate she was awake, and saw your light that night."

A little longer and he was in the drawing-room on a sofa, being petted and spoilt by the Dean and his daughter. There, too, came Lord Castlecomer, his way to Espérance that of a father. He would sit and talk to Harry Wyndham for an hour at a time, making the young man his slave. Sometimes he would thrust an arm through the Dean's, taking him away, and leaving the young people together.

The day came when the invalid was well enough to answer Espérance's question as to how he came to be shut in the cathedral.

"I looked for you as I went out," she said, blushing brightly; "but you were not there."

"You looked for me!" he repeated.

"There were so few who came to evensong," she stammered, in a rosy confusion. "I always knew when you were there. I cannot forgive myself. I ought to have known you had not left. What you must have suffered!"

"You can make up to me for it, Espérance."

He held his arms to her, and, kneeling by him, she laid her head on his breast

The Little Ghost

People touched their foreheads significantly, sighing or smiling, according to their natures, when they spoke of Katharine Venning. She walked through life with something of a scared air—

> Blank misgivings of a creature
> Moving about in worlds not realised.

Just a little bit touched. People stared at her in railway trains or public places, at her great mournful eyes, her strange air of aloofness. Her aunt, Mrs. Constantine, was goodness itself to her.

"Poor Katharine!" she would say. "Who would not be good to her and sorry for her? *What* a fate!"

It was indeed a sad fate. She had gone out to marry her lover, Lawrence Strode, in India. They had waited a long time, and were like happy children at the prospect of re-union. Now that it was to come at last they could hardly wait over the intervening days. People who had travelled with Katharine on that eventful voyage were not likely soon to forget the strange joyousness of her air. Then—it was all over. Lawrence was dead. Hurrying to meet his bride, he had got a touch of sun, heat-apoplexy. He was dead and buried while yet Katharine was a creature beside herself with the joy that was to come.

She took it with a curious quietness. All the way back to England she wondered and wondered how it was that

Lawrence had not come and told her. She was sure she would have done it in his place. She would never have allowed the blow to fall like that. There seemed a strange unreality about it—a mistiness. She had to say over and over to herself, "Lawrence is dead!" and yet the words sounded meaningless. How he had wanted her! Pity tore at her heart for that need of his which had been destined never to be satisfied. Men were unlike women. She had been joyous indeed, but peaceful in anticipating her happiness. He had been tortured with a fear that he would never possess her. Poor Lawrence! Poor fellow!

It was all over years ago. Since those days, by a mere chance, Katharine Venning had become rich. Too late. If the money had come earlier she and Lawrence need never have been parted. She was no longer young, though she had a strange air of youth. You had to look closely at her to discover the little network of fine lines which revealed her age. She was still very slight as to figure, with a suggestion of girlish immaturity even. She had the hovering uncertain air which had been her great charm for the discerning long ago. The little cloud on her brain, so light, so slight that you might have known her for a long time without suspecting it, merely thinking her exotic, unlike other people, had fixed her for ever, it seemed, in innocence and youth.

In the world she was troubled, not part of it. It was cruel to keep her in it with that look of a lost child. Mrs. Constantine, a maternal woman, who had never had a child, during those years in which she had taken care of Katharine had come to love her with a mother's pity. She was pleased when her niece one day, with a deep sigh, as though she were tired, expressed a desire to settle down in a home of her own. They had been wandering about the world for so long restlessly, that it seemed to her as though a good day's rest, the quiet order and routine of a house in English country, would be like Paradise. She wanted to hurry Katharine into shelter.

It had been profanation when people stared at her at the crowded *tables d'hôte*, in the picture galleries, in the churches where Katharine wandered with an absent air. There had been worse things. Katharine kept a curious deceptive loveliness of youth about which Mrs. Constantine had a feeling that, if you touched it, it would fall to dust. She was like the long dead imprisoned in the glaciers who keep their rosiness and the down on their cheek with no suggestion of mortality. Men had fallen in love with Katharine, or had followed her because she was obviously a lady of wealth. It had been to the woman's mind as though they sought a child too young for marriage, or fell in love with the dead. She had had to fly with Katharine many a time, keeping her in ignorance of the cause of the flight. Once she had had to tell the truth to an honest, passionate young Englishman, and to fight against his delusion that his warm love could bring the dead to life. Cedarhurst, when she heard of it, sounded like green fields and founts of refreshment in an arid world.

They might have gone to Katharine's own great house; but there it would not have been the same; the world would not have let them alone. Cedarhurst was in an out-of-the-way corner of the world, tucked under a green hill. It could be managed with few servants. The gardens were charming. High yew hedges, clipped and formal, shut them away. The house, many centuries old, reposed on a green lawn like a dream of peace. It was a house of the old religion to which both Katharine and her aunt belonged. There was a chapel many centuries old, to which an old shaven friar came thrice a week to say mass. The service in the little chapel, with the wind and the sun straying in at the open doors and windows, the ringdoves wheeling and coming in the courtyard without the simple reverent congregation of a few villagers, was heavenly. If the house was old and mouldering, if rats ran in the wainscot, if the old place was worm-eaten through and through, there was yet a sensation of the most lovely cleanness and freshness as of morning dew in the low rooms down the long corridors, where you were always coming upon little shrines with a ruby or a golden lamp burning. It was as though holy and happy people had always inhabited the house. And yet—

Katharine had heard of Cedarhurst from a sympathetic American lady whom they met at Genoa. The idea of it seemed to take possession of her. Within a few hours she had made up her mind to buy it if it was still on the market. The millionaire ship-owner who rented Heron's House, whose heart would be broken if he had to turn out, might sleep in peace.

It was a new Katharine, tense and eager, as they travelled homewards. After years of purposeless existence it was a strange sensation for Mrs. Constantine to sit opposite Katharine in the flying train watching her face with its new expectancy, the light and shadow troubling her eyes as the shadows of clouds a summer field, the small, demure smile of happiness which came and went about her lips.

The loving woman was frightened lest Katharine should be disappointed. It would be terrible if the bird that had suddenly begun to soar after being so long wingless should again fall to earth. She submitted uncomplainingly to the flight homeward, hardly pausing by land or sea. She was dead-tired when at last they reached the friendly Langham, too late for any business to be done. She slept round the clock, and awoke to find Katharine in outdoor things by her bedside.

"Here is your cup of chocolate," she said in a vibrant voice. "Forgive me for waking you. I had to share my news with you. I have been to St. James' Street. Subject to legal delays, Cedarhurst is mine."

Later in the day they travelled down and found the place beyond Mrs. Lesmond's description of it. The hill was over it, and the woods that belonged to the house clothed the hill. There was a lake with water-lilies floating upon it in front of the house, which stood clear of the hill, outside its shadow, if such a green and shining hill could cast a shadow which was not half light. The gardens were full of the singing of birds. There was a pleached alley, a long emerald strip of silk between flower-beds, in their turn intersected by espaliered apple-trees at their coming all rosy. There was a fountain in which a marble boy stood holding an inverted pitcher. It had run dry.

"We shall set it all going again," Katharine said, drawing deep full breaths of happy satisfaction.

"It is bound to be damp, and it is certain to be insanitary," Mrs. Constantine said half humorously; "we may thank our stars there are no drains."

"But acknowledge—it is all wonderfully sweet and restful. We could not have done better," Katharine said, turning to her.

"It is better than one had dared to hope," conceded the elder woman. "All the same, I shall be racked with rheumatism. Those old chintzes; they are certainly heavenly."

Katharine looked about her joyfully. They were in the long, low drawing-room of Cedarhurst. The cedars on the lawn, which gave the place its name, swept with their lower boughs the expanse of shining grass. Something flitted below the boughs of cedar. A sunray. It might have been the golden head of a child.

Katharine peered at it eagerly, her eyes shadowed by her hand. Mrs. Constantine did not know how her niece's heart had leaped in her side.

"It is all adorable," Katharine said. "Isn't it lucky I could buy it just as it stood, with all the dear, lovely old furniture? To think that no one cared about it enough to refuse to sell it. It is our gain. Isn't the china delicious? Come, let us see the bedrooms."

The Little Ghost

She preceded the elder woman up the stairs with a light step, always well in advance of her. They opened a door here and there along the corridors and looked within. Old rooms with great expanses of bare, polished floor, great four-posters set in their midst draped with damask riddled with moth-holes, green and silver, blue and silver, crimson; it was easy to conjecture that the rooms were called from the colour of the damasks. Dim old mirrors glimmered above the mantelpiece; on the faded walls hung old pictures which here and there threw up a high light of scarlet or orange. All was dim, faded, austere.

In one of the room they came upon a picture of a little girl, before which Katharine stood in such an abstraction that Mrs. Constantine had to speak to her several times before she answered. The lady had been exploring a deep, old wardrobe which ran all the side of the room. She came back to Katharine with a speech on her lips which fell silent as she caught the expression of her face. Katharine was standing tip-toe; she was in stature more than common tall; her eyes were lifted to the picture. To the elder woman's imagination she had a flame-like air, as though she were drawn upwards. Her face was terrible and beautiful with love and longing.

Mrs. Constantine's heart sank. Katharine had been so normal of late that she had begun to believe the cloud had passed, or was passing. But plainly nothing except delusion could account for that look in Katharine's eyes, which dwelt upon the portrait of a child, a stiff little figure in a white satin frock, hooped and stayed, the golden head with a string of pearls amid its ringlets. Oddly formal the little figure; but the face not so. The face, bewitchingly full of a roguish mischief, looked straight down. Standing by Katharine's side, Mrs. Constantine had a sudden shock. If Cedarhurst were going to affect one like this, it would be worse than the rheumatism. She had had the delusion that the eyes of the child looked into Katharine's with a living gaze.

"A wonderful thing," she said, taking off her glasses and polishing them. "How the painter has caught the expression! And what a fascinating child—the natural child, despite the way they have bound her up. I should not be surprised now, my dear Katharine, if you had acquired a Van Dyke. The painting of that white satin is marvellous!"

Katharine came back to earth and looked at her with eyes just emerging from dreams. They were beautiful eyes of a strange golden brown, with an introspective air, as though they dwelt much on an unseen world. As she looked at her aunt a shaft of sunlight fell across her face, revealing the innumerable fine wrinkles with which time and grief had fretted it. The skin had a suggestion, in that brief, casual glimpse, of white kid. The beam passed, and she was once again the amazingly youthful Katharine, for whom time might have stood still since her lover's death.

"It is the little child of the house," she said. "The little ghost of the house. Mrs. Lesmond told us—don't you remember?"

"So there is a ghost. No; it was to you Mrs. Lesmond talked. Dear little soul, who could be afraid of her? Has she a name?"

"She has no name—no story, even. I think we will call her Margery. She looks as though she might be Margery."

She left the picture with one last lingering gaze, as though she found it hard to go.

"I shall keep this room for myself," she said. "Margery and I will keep house together. At the top of the house are her nurseries. There have been other children there since. Don't you know? She came and played with them, this little Margery. Grown-up people could not see her; only the children. A nobody's child, I think she had a wicked uncle who did not love her. She was not frightened of him, this little Margery. She was always merry and full of tricks. But she was the little heiress of the house, and so had to be got rid of. I think he murdered her."

Her voice rose to a thin shriek, and Mrs. Constantine was alarmed. The delusions were returning in a more active form. How much Katharine imagined of the child of the house, how much Mrs. Lesmond had told her, she could not be sure. Mrs. Lesmond was a pleasant travelling acquaintance, gone on to her own house in California. They had no address for her. But it would be easy enough to find out presently if there were any such story attached to the little hooped and stayed creature with the roguish eyes.

The storm passed with Katharine quickly as it had arisen. She was happy again, looking back over one shoulder as she ran along an upper corridor with a fleeting and gracious smile. She caught up her long scarf as she ran. In her dress of deep blue she had the grace of a Romney figure.

She paused at the foot of the last flight of stairs and, throwing back her head as though she listened, she looked up. From the lantern overhead the full light fell on her, revealing her cloudy hair dusty upon the fairness. Katharine was growing grey. It came as a shock upon her aunt that one of these days Katharine would be an old woman.

After the pause she ran lightly upstairs. It was a floor of attics, with low beams in the ceilings. They glimmered with a pleasant green dimness through the open doors. They were almost furnitureless, and one or two were full of lumber. Katharine passed them by as though she knew the place.

"These are the nurseries," she said, opening a door and passing within.

Her short-sighted eyes peered in the corners and found nothing. She glanced at the great old doll's house as high as the room itself, in which a child might hide; at the heavy carved wooden bed, a child's bed, carved with rough, tender little faces of children. Cupboards ran round the walls with dim paintings in the panels. She passed them by and hurried into the inner room. Nothing at all there. Only a bird twittered to its young in the screen of green leaves that was drawn over all the windows.

While they stood side by side looking about them, something sounded close at hand—the mischievous laugh of a child. So irresistible was it that Mrs. Constantine started and looked around, half expecting a warm and laughing face in the doorway; but there was nothing. A delusion, surely, born of the old house and the dimness and the things they had been talking of. But Katharine's face was irradiated.

"You heard?" she said in a tone of soft delight. "I never looked for it that she should come so soon. Little sweetheart! she knows how lonely I am for the child that might have been mine and Laurie's, if only we had not waited."

She would not hear of returning to town. She would sleep at the inn at the entrance to the forest, while they got the servants down and made the place habitable. Mrs. Constantine was at her wits' end. There was a good deal that needed doing to the old place. Katharine, asserting herself as the mistress, would have as little done as possible; harassed the workmen while the little was adoing; seemed as though she could not sleep or rest till they had Cedarhurst to themselves; was ever afoot between the inn and the house till the last workman had packed up his tools and departed.

An old priest with a shaven crown came tramping over from his monastery at Lyte, reading his breviary as he came slowly under the arches of the summer trees. He was to offer Mass once or twice a week in the chapel at Cedarhurst, and was rejoiced that the house had been bought by an adherent of the old religion. He was a beneficent old man, and after he had sat and talked with the two ladies for a little while he suggested that he should bless the house.

"An old Catholic custom," he said; "you will wish to observe it?"

"It will not—it will not," said Katharine stammering, "frighten away . . . perhaps a little ghost . . . if there should be such a thing?"

"Margery Ferrars," he said, smiling peacefully and taking snuff. "No, the blessing will not frighten away that innocent. The house has been blessed before without banishing Margery. But, indeed, if I knew the words that would send her to Heaven, I would say them."

"Oh no, you would not—you would not! What would the house be without Margery?" Katharine broke out. "It would be cruel—cruel!"

He looked at her in surprise.

"A little white soul," he said. "What does it do flitting about 'twixt earth and heaven? Who would not give it rest if he could?"

She wrung her hands in her lap, and her face looked frightened to death.

"She will be happy with me," she said, as though she pleaded for dear life. "Indeed, she will be happy."

"There is no happiness, my child, like the happiness of Heaven to the Christian soul," he said with a benign gentleness; and added that if God permitted little Margery to wander on earth, it must be for His own good purpose.

So the tense hour passed. Mrs. Constantine walked with Father Bernard to the gate by which he emerged from Cedarhurst into the forest. She wanted to explain about Katharine; the tragedy of her life, which had left so sad a result behind; her obsession of Margery Ferrars.

"Of late years I have noticed," she said, blushing slightly over her rosy, pretty old face, "that my niece has become passionately fond of children. I think she sees in every child just a glimpse of the child that might have been hers if she had married poor Mr. Strode. It has made her happy to be with them, and yet unhappy, for they are always some other woman's and not hers. You will not smile, Father, when I tell you that, some time ago, she bought a big doll and took to nursing it when she was alone. I was dreadfully afraid of ridicule for the poor darling. My life is devoted to standing between the unthinking world and Katharine. Since we came to Cedarhurst she has forgotten the doll. It lies upstairs at the top of the play-cupboard, in what Katharine calls the nursery. I do not dare give it away lest she should ask for it; but she seems to have forgotten it completely. You believe in the ghost of Margery Ferrars, Father?"

"I do not dare to disbelieve the many innocent children who have said that they saw it. Many years ago a lady who lived here with one delicate little boy—Lady Leuthwaite—sent for me because she was in trouble about her son Archie. He either pretended a playmate, or he had an invisible one. We sat and watched the boy at his play. He was about five years old. He certainly played with something—somebody we could not see. A mischievous playmate, too. He had built a tower of bricks with great care. Suddenly it was swept over; and there certainly was a sound like a child's mischievous laugh. Little Archie scolded—something. He put his knuckles in his eyes and wept! Something—we could not see—consoled him. In a minute or two he was laughing and building the tower again. And—something helped him. We saw the bricks placed by an invisible hand."

Mrs. Constantine was pale and agitated.

"My niece is fitting up the nurseries as for a living child. She writes to London for everything a child could fancy, and puts it in place herself. She has made the nurseries her sitting-rooms. I have gone up there and found her sewing—she does a deal of fine, exquisite work for poor churches and poor children. She has not been alone, though I could see nothing. I have heard Katharine laugh as I went up the stairs, as I have not heard her laugh since Lawrence Strode died. And—I don't know what to make of such a thing. Our little ghost plays pranks—such things as a child might do. Hannah, the housemaid, complained to me the other day that the new young footman laid a booby trap for her. A sponge soaked in water fell on her head as she went into Katharine's room in the morning. Edward denied it indignantly. I believe the boy. The bells ring when no one has touched them. I found the whole contents of my work-box on the floor yesterday, my precious mother-o'-pearl bobbins spilt in every direction. I was nearly sure that I heard a laugh as I stooped to pick them up. Is the old house full of nerves that one believes such things?"

"They are characteristic of Margery," Father Bernard said with the tender look of one who adores children when he discusses them. "It was the same in Lady Leuthwaite's time. I remember that her ladyship told us that she was always finding silk threads tangling about her feet. Once she was sure that a pair of soft hands were clasped upon her eyes as her candle went out, leaving her in the dark. She was not at all afraid. But she was afraid for Archie, so she gave up Cedarhurst and went to live in a new house where there were no 'ghosts'."

"Katharine feeds on the little ghost's presence and grows well liking and almost rosy—for her," Mrs. Constantine said with a sigh. "Poor child—as long as she is happy . . . "

The summer turned round to winter, and the spring came again; and Katharine Venning, who had been overthin, came to have a certain matronly beauty and ripeness in her look. She sang to herself now as she went up and down the stairs or walked in the gardens, always with a suggestion of a little hand thrust in hers and a little face looking up to meet the tender brooding of her gaze.

They had few visitors. Mrs. Constantine excused her niece to callers, pleading that she was an invalid; and the excuse passed because Katharine kept to the garden and grounds of Cedarhurst. Except for her obsession of Margery Ferrars, she seemed quite normal. No one seeing her with her elegant and gracious air of the mistress could believe that there was anything amiss. The romps with the invisible playmate were conducted with so mouselike a quietness that not even the servants took fright. And Katharine's physical health was certainly wonderfully improved. The maturity of beauty denied her so long, coming late as it did, was like the awakening of youth from its grave. Time had been when Mrs. Constantine had seen age approach her beautiful Katharine—the age which shrinks and withers and makes lean. Now she rubbed her eyes. The expanding beauty of wifehood and motherhood had come to Katharine. The dust on her stately head now became her. Who could think of age in contemplation of such fresh bloom?

"I do not like the cedar-tree on the lawn," Katharine said one day, turning about on the piano-stool to look at Mrs. Constantine. Her long fingers rested on the keys. The angel sleeves of her gown—one of the beautiful blues she liked to wear—swept the ground at her feet. She had an odd sensation to Mrs. Constantine's eyes of St. Cecilia at the organ. "I do not like the cedar-tree on the lawn," she said, and her voice complained. "I thought it would be such a good place to play hide-and-seek with Margery, but when we come there she always vanishes. I thought at first it was only play, but she does not come again, not for hours."

"There are plenty of places as well as the cedar-tree," Mrs. Constantine said, as though she spoke to a child. She was wondering to herself what such and such an one of her old unimaginative daylight world would think of this mad life in which Margery Ferrars came and went like any living inmate of the house.

"There is one thing about Margery," Katharine said another day: "she will never grow up. She will always be just the sweet age she is now—just six years old." She quoted Wordsworth softly to herself:

> A six-years' Darling of a pigmy size,
> Fretted by sullies of his Mother's kisses,
> With light upon him from his Father's eyes.

"Poor Margery!" she went on. "She had no mother to kiss her till I came. I wonder who will mother her when I am dead?"

She fixed her mournful eyes on Mrs. Constantine's face; and for once the lady had no comfort to offer.

The winter turned round to February—a strange February, grey and warm, with many sudden storms. Night after night, at the end of the calm day, the wind got up and blew a gale. Sometimes lightenings flashed outside the shuttered windows. Uncanny weather, and it seemed alternately to excite and depress Katharine. She slept ill at nights and wandered about the house, coming to the breakfast-table in the morning with heavy eyes.

When the tornado broke on the twenty-third of the month, she kept vigil with the rest of the house while it was at its worst, slipping away now and again from the lit drawing-room, where they tried to shut out the sounds of the elemental fury of Nature, and going upstairs to the nursery, where of late she had had her bed removed, to the mystification of the well-trained servants.

"Margery sleeps well," she said with her finger to her lips, as her aunt, following her, surprised her leaning above the little old carved bed with the heads of angel-children in the panels.

"I wish you did, my darling. You look frightfully tired. What a night! It is the storm of a lifetime. Fortunately Cedarhurst is sound."

Towards morning the storm lessened and Katharine consented to lie down in her own bed, where she lay with her face turned towards the child's bed. She fell asleep, and in the grey dawn which was revealing the rack and ruin outside, Mrs. Constantine found her sleeping, her hand extended from under the bedclothes clasping, it might be, a little hand. It might have been the cold, grey light, but lying asleep there her new bloom seemed to have departed. She looked shrunken and sad and grey, and the dust on her hair showed as though it were snow.

She slept late and long. Mrs. Constantine was glad she slept. For something strange had happened. The cedar-tree was down, its branches sprawling against the house-wall, where it had brought down part of a chimney-stack. The old roots were torn out of the ground, leaving a great pit where they had been. There had come up with them the coffin and bones of a little child.

Mrs. Constantine, as though it were a matter of life and death, sent a hasty messenger for Father Bernard. He came as fast as he could and blessed a little spot of earth, and with the prayers he laid the bones to rest till the Judgement Day. Quietly as he had come he departed. A little handful of dust of a child centuries dead. What had anyone to do with it? He laid the child to rest, and none was the wiser except himself and Mrs. Constantine.

"It would not be safe for Katharine to know," she said in agitated whispers, as they returned to the house after the strange little ceremony. "Supposing the child should come no more?"

"God is good," said the old priest. "It is innocence to innocence."

The little ghost came no more, and, after the first restless days of seeking her, Katharine became so dull and listless that Mrs. Constantine was frightened. At last Father Bernard told her the truth—how the little bones had been discovered and laid at rest in consecrated ground.

"Think of her as playing in Heaven with Our Lady's beads," he said, "and the youngest angels for playfellows"; and the old face was wise and tender. "How merry it will be there! Do you think God, who made children, would be satisfied with a Heaven in which there was neither laughter nor the pranks of a child?"

Katharine seemed to take comfort. She was very quiet and gentle and reasonable, having made up her mind that Margery would come no more, being too happy where she was to care to leave it. Nevertheless, her age had suddenly come upon her, and more than her age, for it was evident that she was fading fast. No doctor or doctor's stuff could keep her who seemed almost overwilling to be gone.

She died one night in her sleep after a few days during which the flame of life had burnt up so rosily that poor Mrs. Constantine, who had been bemoaning her fate that she must be left and her child taken, was deluded into fond hopes that she might turn her face earthwards again.

It was Mrs. Constantine who found her just as the shadows were fleeing before the golden spears of the dawn. While she stood at the foot of the bed, becoming slowly aware of the silence in which there was no breathing but her own, she saw, or thought she saw, a strange thing. Katharine lay turned partly on her right side. Her arm was extended in the attitude of a woman who nurses a baby at her breast. There was a child lying within the arm, a golden head against the breast. Then the sunlight stole into the room. There was nothing, only Katharine Venning, with the age and the sorrow smoothed out of her face.

The Little Ghost

The stars began to peep;
   Gone was the bitter day;
She heard the milky ewes
   Bleat to their lambs astray.
Her heart cried for her lamb
   Cold in the churchyard sod:
She could not think on the happy children
   At play with the Lamb of God.

She heard the calling ewes
   And the lambs' answer, alas!
She heard her heart's blood drip in the night
   As the ewes' milk on the grass.
Her tears that burnt like fire
   So bitter and slow ran down:
She could not think on the new-washed children
   Playing by Mary's down.

Oh, who is this come in
   Over her threshold-stone?
And why is the old dog wild with joy
   Who all day long made moan?
This fair little radiant ghost,
   Her one little son of seven,
New-'scaped from the band of merry children
   In the nurseries of Heaven.

The Little Ghost

He was all clad in white,
 Without a speck of stain;
His curls had a ring of light
 That rose and fell again.
"Now come with me, my own mother,
 And you shall have great ease,
For you shall see the lost children
 Gathered to Mary's knees."

Oh, lightly sprang she up,
 Nor waked her sleeping man;
And hand in hand with the little ghost
 Through the dark night she ran.
She is gone swift as a fawn,
 As a bird homes to its nest.
She has seen them lie, the sleepy children,
 'Twixt Mary's arm and breast.

At morning she came back;
 Her eyes were strange to see.
She will not fear the long journey
 However long it be.
As she goes in and out
 She sings unto hersel';
For she has seen the mother's children
 And knows that it is well.

The Picture on the Wall

"Upon my word, Millicent"—with an impatient laugh—"there are times I could swear your heart wasn't in it; times when, for all your childlike transparency, I could almost believe there was another man somewhere to whom you had given all that ought to be mine."

"Oh, hush, hush," answered a soft voice; "don't say such things my darling; they are treason against our love."

"Poor little woman," said the man repentantly. "I oughtn't to have said that, for I know it is not true. But you are cold-blooded, little girl—deucedly cold-blooded. Here have I been talking about our honeymoon—our honeymoon that you seem so determined to postpone—and cheating myself by talking of it into a half-belief that it had arrived, and yet, when I look in those milky eyes of yours to see if I have put a spark of fire into them, I find only a wandering look of alarm. Is it any wonder you baffle and distress me?"

The girl lifted up the eyes he had called milky. The unusual epithet was the right one in her case. The wide innocent-looking eyes were of a curious pale blue, nearer the colour of spilt milk than anything else one could think of. There was a slightly scared expression about them, and the sensitive lines of the mouth, the fineness of the silky hair, the frequent movements of the slender hands, all spoke of a highly-strung, nervous organisation.

"I am afraid," she said, "with me love means fear. You are so strong and confident. While I, since I have known and

The Picture on the Wall

loved you, I have realised with anguish the thousand and one chances that may snatch us away from each other for ever."

"The more reason for hastening, my white rose, despite your too active imagination—I should scarcely breathe till we belonged to each other. After that the deluge."

The girl trembled violently within his arms, murmuring his name half inaudibly.

" 'Geoffrey, Geoffrey,' " he repeated after her. "But what have I said to frighten you, my sweetheart? Nothing can separate us. It is only your timidity that delays our heaven. Why, Millicent, why? Do you know sometimes I could crush you to bend your will to mine? What a will, little girl, though you look so soft and yielding!"

"I will yield everything once we are married, Geoffrey!"

"Yes, darling," said the man, suddenly mollified; "but when is that to be?"

"Let us forget about it, Geoffrey, for a little while. Let us be lovers. Marriage so often means the end of love, or, at least, the end of romance."

"It shall not with us, you foolish child. I promise you that, if that is all you fear."

She gave a little tired sigh as of one who gives in out of weariness.

"Poor Geoffrey," she said, stroking his cheek. "It is hard that you should be worried with my inexplicable whims. Wait a little longer patiently. When you come to Dormer Court next month I promise you that then I will fix the date—if you still desire it."

The man laughed.

"If I still desire it, sweetheart! Well, thanks, for so much grace. I have had visions of your perpetual unwillingness that should land us somewhere into old age unmarried."

The girl crept closer to him and they were silent—the silence of lovers that means so much satisfaction. After a time they stood up and sauntered easily down the garden path. It was September, and the late roses were out in bloom, and now and again a bird trilled sweetly, a little song very different from the full rapture of early summer.

> *"The latest of late warblers sings as one*
> *That trolls at random when the feast is over."*

quoted Millicent Gray.

The homely red house came into sight, with its verandah, and the many garden paths diverging from it into winding walk and shrubbery. There was a lady in the verandah, comfortably seated in a rocking-chair, her eyes bent on the novel in her hand, and a pretty tea equipage drawn within reach of her. She looked up as the lovers approached.

"Dear people," she said gaily, "I am glad you have thought at last of me and the tea. I have had some difficulty in restraining Jones's impatience. Though, indeed, if I had taken my tea a quarter of an hour ago, and given you the tannin, I don't suppose you would be a whit the wiser."

She tinkled a little bell at her elbow, and in a minute or two the spruce Jones arrived with the teapot. Mrs. Evelyn drew herself up from her languid position and poured out the tea. She was an exceedingly pretty woman, nut-brown and with flashing white teeth, this cousin of Geoffrey Annesley and school-friend of his betrothed.

"Well, Helen," said Annesley, "we haven't been idle. Millicent has at least named a time for naming the time for our marriage. Most men mightn't think it a tremendous concession, but I am grateful for small favours."

"She's a shy bird, Geoffrey," Mrs. Evelyn answered, getting up to kiss her friend. "So I think you have gained a concession. And Millicent is well worth waiting for. But here comes my great boy!" she cried, as the house door was opened by a smiling nurse, and a delightful brown-faced youngster toddled on to the and ran to his mother.

"Thank you, Nurse," she said. "Now you go to your tea while I take care of Master John."

The boy trotted from his mother to Millicent, and stood by her knee, leaning his chubby arms upon her dress. Presently the two went down on the lawn for a romp—a delightful romp—with a ball and a puppy, which was accompanied by peals of laughter.

"She will make an exquisite mother some day," said Mrs. Evelyn, translating into words something of the look in the man's eyes.

He gave her a swift glance which had a shy gratitude in it.

"I am nearly tired of waiting, Helen," he said. "She is in no great hurry to give me my happiness."

"But she was promised something now?"

"She has promised to fix a date when I go down next month to their place. Have you ever been there, Helen?"

"Never. For all our staunch friendship, Millicent has always had her reserves with me. I know little about her family except that they are poor and proud."

"The father's letter to me was stiff enough. I suppose they live in a kind of feudal atmosphere in their Northumbrian woods. I might have resented the tone of it, only I feel so unworthy of my girl. After all, if the old fellow writes as if he were of the blood royal, I, Millicent's lover, should be the last to complain."

"You have the ideal temper for a lover."

"It has been sorely tried, Helen. I assure you. You women wear well through an indefinite engagement. For some incredible reason you made your heyday of it; while with us it is a time that stirs the sleeping savage in us more than any other set of circumstances in which we could be placed."

"Poor Geoffrey! But here comes your pretty lady-love. And my young savage has pulled down all the gold-silver of her hair. How delightful she looks dishevelled!"

It was indeed a charming face that looked at them as Millicent came towards them, vainly endeavouring to twist up the coil the child had pulled about her shoulders.

September passed goldenly, and the trees were full pomp when there came in wild weather with the October new moon. The storms very soon made havoc of garden and woodland, and every day brought tidings of destruction by land and sea. It was on one of those wild days that Geoffrey Annesley and Millicent Gray left King's Cross for the long journey northwards. It was murky in the great station, and without in the yellow streets there was a fog of rain, and a sodden splashing under foot where the miserable ranks of pedestrians trudged stolidly.

The lovers were undismayed by the weather. Millicent for once seemed to have pitched care to the winds, and her eyes had a brighter light, her cheeks a rosier flush than usual.

When the train steamed out, and they were rushing through grey sheets of water, past ghosts of warehouses and ranges of dingy dwellings, dimly seen through the mist, Geoffrey leant forward and took the two little hands warm from the muff. They were alone in the compartment.

"This might be our honeymoon, little woman," he said, fondling the slim fingers.

"In this weather?" she asked.

"Yes; why not? I should have no eyes for the weather."

"Nor I," she said, softly audacious.

"No, sweet?" he cried delightedly. "So you wish for the dreaded time, after all?"

"*Wish* for it! Ah, that is a poor way of putting it."

He had not often seen her in this mood, and was enchanted.

"You are making up to me now for being so cold sometimes. You have starved me, Millicent. You women don't know what it is never to meet with an answering ardour."

"I have never felt cold even when I seemed so. I have been afraid to show you all I felt. Believe this, my dear. But to-day I am done with fear. No matter what comes you must believe in the fullness of my love for you."

The rain lasted all day till late evening, when the lights of a little wayside station shone blurred through the mist.

They drove to Dormer Court through a heavily wooded country. The place looked ancient, and did, indeed, date back some hundreds of years. The dining-hall was panelled with fine old oak, and the fireplaces on each side massively carved. A gallery ran round it, from which corridors diverged each side to the sleeping apartments. There was a good deal of armour in the shadowy corners, and on the high dresser there was a show of heavy silver plate, the sale of which might have turned the poverty of the Gray family to affluence. But Sir Roland Gray would as soon have thought of selling one of his daughters, perhaps sooner, as of reducing the heritage that had come to him by turning the slightest portion of it into hard cash.

He was a frosty old gentleman, with a haughty air which Annesley did not find reassuring. Dormer Court seemed to him a rather chilly place, and, glancing at Millicent as they entered, he thought she looked suddenly nervous and depressed. Those great fireplaces would have needed roaring cressets of wood in them to make the place human, but they showed only polished brass dogs, evidently quite innocent of use—for some time, at least.

Annesley noticed these things as he passed through the hall on his way to the drawing-room, an apartment as stately as the dining-hall, and more chilly. There Millicent's sister and his hostess awaited them. She was a rather unhappy-looking woman, past her first youth and delicate-looking.

His room, to which he followed a manservant carrying his portmanteau, was gloomy. The bed had huge testers hung with heavy curtains; the shuttered windows were also heavily draped; the dark mahogany furniture was of the most massive build. But as soon as the servant had left the room, and Annesley had an opportunity to notice these things, he observed a portrait above the fireplace which seemed to dominate the room, and which drew his own gaze to it with a curious sense of fascination.

The portrait was that of a handsome man, dressed according to the period of the second Charles. His skin had the peculiarly warm ruddy tinge we associate with Vandyck's portraits, and out of this setting his eyes looked startlingly blue. His love-locks straying over a steel corselet were golden brown, and altogether he looked a most gallant cavalier. But the paintings of the eyes was the painter's great achievement. As Annesley stood looking at the picture with a candle lighted the better to see it, he could have sworn the eyes looked back at him like those of a living man. He turned to the dressing-table with a half-uneasy laugh at his own delusion. He had laughed out unconsciously, and as he did so he thought that laugh was faintly echoed within the room. He looked around him sharply, No, the room looked harmless enough, and it was not likely to be anything but imagination. Yet the eyes of the portrait seemed to gaze towards him, and he fancied now that they had a saturnine gleam in them.

"Nerves, my friend," he muttered to himself. "This is a new development. You'll be looking under the bed and prodding the window-curtains for burglars next, like any hysterical woman."

But he could not shake off the sense of being watched. He made a resolution not to yield to his folly by looking at the portrait, but as he went to and fro he felt assured that the eyes were following him.

"Confound you, sir" he said at last, half jocosely, "I wish you'd keep your eyes out of my back."

He could have sworn again that he heard the faint, malicious laugh.

"Well," he said as he finished his toilet, "if Dormer Court possesses such a thing as a haunted room, I'm in it. It would make a nice little case for the Psychical Society."

At dinner the conversation somewhat flagged. Annesley did his best valiantly to keep it going, but reflected within himself that certainly Dormer Court was not cheerful. Millicent had become very quiet since she entered her home, and Sir Roland, though he treated his guest with very punctilious courtesy, had apparently little to say; the elder Miss Gray scarcely spoke, and once when Annesley addressed her directly started violently.

"Poor little Millicent!" said the lover to himself. "No wonder she is a little strange sometimes. She will be different in a happier atmosphere."

Presently, in the search for a subject of conversation, he remembered the portrait.

"That is a very fine portrait over the fireplace in my bedroom. A genuine Vandyck, is it not, Sir Roland?"

The baronet bent his frosty brows upon him.

"It is not a Vandyck," he said coldly.

Millicent had turned quite pale when the picture was mentioned. She now leant forward, and said in a shocked voice:

"You have not put him in that room, father?"

"Why not?" said the old man sharply. "Guests of honour have slept in that room many a time."

The girl sank back in her seat very pale. Annesley had no opportunity later of asking the meaning of this odd little scene. He guessed, indeed, that the room had some ill name, but was not perturbed. The man in the portrait was a decent looking fellow, he thought, and if he chose to walk, why, one might have worse company. He was not at all likely to be afraid of a ghost; indeed, to see one was an experience he rather coveted, for he had had most other adventures that can fall to a civilised man.

The evening was no improvement on the dinner. Millicent sat silent and scared-looking. Her sister played melancholy music at the grand piano, and Sir Roland, having detained the young man inordinately long in the dining-room, discussing some dry aspect of politics which happened to interest him, continued the discussion till ten o'clock, at which hour everyone was expected to retire. By ten o'clock Annesley was indeed in rather a bad temper. He didn't like his future father-in-law, with his bushy eyebrows, his pursed, opinionated mouth, and his light eyes, with their suggestion of evil temper.

"Once I carry off my girl," he said to himself, " 'tis precious little Dormer Court will see of us."

He had nothing but a handshake of her at parting for the night. Into that, however, he managed to infuse as much loving reassurance as he could under her father's discouraging glance. When he went up to his room he again examined the portrait. The life-likeness of the eyes was so pronounced that he reached up to feel the painted canvas, and so make sure. He was reminded of a story he had once read, in which someone had been spied upon by living eyes gazing through the holes where the painted eyes of the portrait had been.

"Only harmless canvas!" he said to himself; "but the painter of those eyes, if he wasn't Vandyck, must have had an uncanny sort of genius of his own."

He determined to look no more at the portrait, but blew out his candle and jumped into bed. He was soon sleeping soundly, in spite of the rain that beat against the windows, and the blast that howled in the chimney.

He could not have told how long he had slept when he was awakened by a cold breath on his forehead. He opened his eyes in thick darkness, and thrust out his hands; they met only the air, though that struck strangely chill. Then from the dark into which he gazed a face shaped itself—an evil face, swollen, distorted, malignant; the eyes, with a red gleam in them, looked furiously into his. Annesley was a brave man, but the hair of his head stood up, and the sweat came in drops on his forehead. He pushed both hands against the face, and felt nothing, but it seemed to recede a little into the darkness. Then, still watching it, he felt for the box of matches which had stood beside his bed. He scarcely knew how he was able to see the face, because he felt the darkness of the room to be intense; the light seemed to come in some strange way from the apparition itself, and to illumine only that.

He struck a match sharply, and the flame sputtered a little, and then stood up steadily. The face was gone now. He jumped out of bed and lit the candles on his dressing-table. Then he peered about him into the dark corners. There was nothing. He opened the great wardrobe, looked behind curtains, lifted the valance of the bed. There was nothing anywhere. He sat down on the side of his bed and wiped his face.

"By Jove!" he said; "that *was* a nasty experience!"

He lifted his eyes to the portrait. The eyes were still watching him, and he had the delusion that their expression had changed. They looked like the eyes of an enemy. The eyes of the apparition—he shuddered recalling them—had the expression of a tiger before he springs. Annesley felt with a sick horror that another minute of darkness, and the creature would have grappled with him.

He was struck now by a certain likeness between the eyes of the portrait and those tiger-eyes. And the face—yes, there had been a shadowy likeness. If the handsome face there on the wall had been battered, bruised, beaten out of human likeness, it might be something like that face in the dark.

Annesley looked at his watch: one o'clock. The room was very cold, and smelt damp. He was determined not to lie down again in the canopied bed, where he had seemed so horribly at the mercy of the evil thing. He looked around for materials to make a fire. There were none. A fire would have been companionable in his vigil. He looked at his two candles. They were tall and solid, and would last till daylight. He wished he had had a book to keep him company, for he was determined not to sleep again; but the most diligent search in the room brought him nothing, and he remembered, with an impatient exclamation, that he had left his big parcel of newspapers in the hall as he entered.

He dressed himself fully, and then threw himself in an arm-chair to get through the hours as best he could. He had deliberately turned the chair so that he should not see the portrait. How he wished for some companionship in his dreary vigil; if only he had Jim, his bulldog, whom he had left forlorn behind him in London! He gazed at the candles steadily while the slow minutes passed. When he thought half an hour had gone he looked at his watch. It was only ten minutes past one. If he had been more at home in the house he would have left that unpleasant room and betaken himself anywhere, out in the storm even. But he had the English dislike of doing anything out of the ordinary, and when he contemplated an escape from the house he imagined a midnight alarm, and all the consequent rumpus.

He must have dozed in his chair, for he awoke in a cold sweat suddenly, with that clammy breath lifting the hair on his forehead, and an ice-cold hand on his throat. When he sprang into wakefulness the hand slowly relaxed its grasp. There was nothing to be seen except that the candles were guttering in the wind from the chimney.

He flung back the window shutters and opened the windows. He thought now of the room as of a grave. The fresh air rushing in seemed to steady him. His heart was beating fast, and he could not rid himself of a conviction that those fingers had meant to strangle him. The rest of the night and during the grey dawn he walked up and down his room.

The morning brought relief, and also anger. He was in no state of mind to unravel the things that had happened to him, but he was furious at the house and the people. That old devil, as he mentally called Sir Roland, must have known what guests that infernal room of his harboured, and yet had put him there to sleep. And Millicent—she had let him sleep there.

His anger became cold, but none the less steady, at the thought of her.

But the bitter things he could have said in his first brief anger froze on his lips when they met. He was early in the breakfast-room, and had packed his portmanteau for his departure before coming downstairs. But she was waiting for him. A great rush of pity flowed into his heart as he saw her. She looked so pale, so forlorn, so utterly hopeless and wretched. And he had been thinking of her as sleeping well!

He went towards her with a half-articulate expression of tenderness.

"No," she said, waving him back, "not now. Come this way, we shall be disturbed here, and I must speak to you."

She led the way to a little room that opened off the hall.

"This is my own room, where no one comes unless I ask them," she said. "We are safe here. Now tell me, my dear, how did the night go?"

Her voice was full of tenderness, but it was a tenderness that repelled rather than attracted. He felt that she wanted no lover-like demonstrations, and that the few feet of space between them might have been as wide as the sea, so effectually did she seem to set him apart.

"You know," he said awkwardly by way of answer, "I did not sleep well."

The Death Spancel

"You saw *it*?" she asked, her eyes dilating.

"I certainly fancied I saw something very unpleasant."

"Don't try to describe it," she said. "Go back to the room. Lift the picture over the fireplace and look at the reverse side. Then come back here and tell me if that is what you saw."

"He obeyed dumbly. The portrait was a heavy one to lift, but his arms were strong, and he swung it around on its cord. When it turned into the light he almost cried out. On the back of the portrait was painted the face he had seen in the night.

He hurried from the room with a shudder. He felt that he never wanted to enter it again, and his repugnance to the house was so strong that he could hardly breathe within its four walls. He returned to where he had left her.

"Well?" she said.

"I don't know what devilry is at the root of it, but the face on the back of the portrait is the face that came to me in the night."

For a minute she hid her eyes. Then she spoke in a voice which pain had made apathetic.

"It is the end of our love."

He would have uttered a fierce protest, but she silenced him with a commanding gesture.

"It is the end, and nothing you can ever say or do will make it otherwise. The man on the wall, whose evil spirit still haunts that room, was an ancestor—Sir Anthony Gray. He was a bad man, and after a wicked life he died raving mad. Whether the second portrait of him in this madness was painted cynically or seriously none of us know. Its existence is only known to ourselves. Unhappily, Sir Anthony left us his madness. Now and then it skips a generation; my father escaped, but our only brother is a dangerous madman, and at any time the curse may seize upon Alison or me. I was wicked when I thought I could marry you and keep this from you, but not wicked enough to do it with a light heart. You will some day be grateful for the night of terror that saved you from a worse thing. I shall never marry now, and I only hope that you will be able to forgive me, because I loved you and was sorely tempted."

"I will not give you up," said the man with an oath.

"You will," she said sadly. "You will be sad for a little while, but presently you will realise what an escape you have had, and be glad."

"Millicent, Millicent, are you in earnest? Am I really to go away out of your life, and you out of mine?"

There was a despair in his cry, but there was also acquiescence, and she caught the sound. She looked at his imploring face with a maternal pity.

"It must be, my dear," she said.

"I will wait for you," he cried. "I shall never marry, and I shall always be ready to come to you. Oh, Millicent, Millicent, is there no help?"

But even as he said it he knew there was none. The reeling shock of the thing, cornering upon him after his night of terror, had scarcely left him the power of thinking clearly, but somewhere at the back of his mind he was conscious that what she had told him was irrevocable. However, his wounded passion cried out for her, he felt that her most unhappy doom had set her as far beyond man's love as though she were already dead.

"Good-bye," she said mournfully; but she did not offer to kiss him or to touch his hand. "The carriage will be round for you presently, and you will wait till it comes. I shall explain to my father, for you will not care to see him."

She left him standing there, dumb, and glided like a ghost from the room. A few minutes later the servant brought him his coffee on a tray, with a message that the carriage was ready. He drank the coffee half-consciously, thinking to himself that she had not been so lost in her bitter trouble as to forget his material wants. Millicent had always been kind; he remembered that her kindness was one of the qualities he had loved in her.

A minute later the carriage had swept him into the depths of the forest. Millicent Gray, unseen herself, watched it depart, and noticed that his head was bowed and his shoulders drooped. It was her last sight of him. As the forest took him she turned away to accept the burden of her lonely life, and the terrible possibilities it held.

The Fields of My Childhood

They lie far away, gray with the mists of memory, under a veil of distance, half-silver, half-gold, like the gossamer, so far that they might never have been save only in dreams. They are not nearly so real as the Eastern world of the stories I read yesterday, but I know where they lie—common fields nowadays, and seldom visited. Yet, there was a child once who knew every inch of them as well as the ant her anthill, or the silvery minnow her brown well under the stone cover, to which one descends by ancient water-stained steps.

The fields are there, but their face somewhat changed, as other things are changed. We were little ones when we came to live among them, in a thatched house full of little nests of rooms, the walls of which were run over by flowery trellises that made them country-like even by candle-light. Of candle-light I have not much memory, for we went to bed in the gloaming, when the long, long day had burned itself out and the skies were washed with palest green that held the evening star; and we slept dreamlessly till the golden day shot through the chinks of the shutters, and we leapt to life again with a child's zest for living. At the back of the house there was an overgrown orchard, a dim, delicious place where the gnarled boughs made a roof against heaven. It was our adventure, time and again, to escape through our windows and wash our feet in the May dew before we were discovered. One whole summer, indeed, these revels were hindered by a bull which was pastured on the lush herbage. But how entrancing it was to hear him roar at night, close by our bed's head, or to see his great shadow cross the chink of moonlight in the shutter! Sometimes he ate the rose-bushes that wreathed our window, and, rubbing his gigantic flanks against the house-wall, bellowed, while we shook in bed in delicious tremors, and imagined our cosy nest a tent in the African desert, with lions roaring outside. I remember the rooms so well: the chilly parlour, only used when we had grown-up visitors, for we were there in charge of a nurse; the red-tiled kitchen, with its settle and its little windows opening inward; the door that gave on a grass-grown approach; and the stone seat outside, where we sat to shell peas, or made "plays" with broken bits of crockery and the shreds of shining tin pared by the travelling tinker when he mended the porringers. I remember the very cups and saucers from which we drank our rare draughts of tea—delicate china, with sea-shells on it in tones of gray, the varied shapes of which gave us ever-new interest.

As I look back, I can never see that house in unwinking daylight, though it was perpetual summer then, and never a rainy day. Rooms and passages are always dim with a subdued green light, the reflection, I suppose, through the narrow windows wreathed with verdure, and from the grass and the plaited apple-boughs. But the spirit of improvement has laid all waste, has thrown the wee rooms into ample ones, has changed the narrow windows for bays and oriels, has thinned the apple-trees for the sake of the grass. There was once a pond, long and green, with a little island in the midst, where a water-hen had her nest. I always thought of it as the pond in Hans Andersen's *Ugly Duckling*, and never watched the ducks paddling among the reeds that I did not look to the sky to see the wild geese, that were contemptuously friendly with the poor hero, flecking the pearl-strewn blue. The pond

The Fields of My Childhood

is filled up now with the macadam of a model farmyard. Iron and stone have replaced the tumble-down yellow sheds, where we drank sheep's milk in a gloom powdered with sun-rays; the two shrubberies have gone, and the hedge of wild roses that linked the trees in the approach to the house. Naught remains save the thatched roof, many feet deep, the green porch over the hall door, the stone seat round the streaky apple-tree at the garden gate, and the garden itself, where the largest lilies I have ever seen stand in the sun, and the apple-trees are in the garden-beds, the holly-hocks elbow the gooseberries, and the violets push out their little clumps in the celery-bed.

But the fields. It is only to the ignorant all fields are the same; as there are some who see no individualities in animals because they have no heart for them. Here and there hedges have been levelled and dykes filled, and now their places are marked by a long dimple in the land's face. The well in the midst of one has been filled up, despite the warning of an old mountain farmer that ill-luck would surely follow whosoever demolished the fairy well. Over it grew a clump of briar and thorn-trees, where one found the largest, juiciest blackberries; that too is gone, but, practically, the fields remain the same. There is the Ten Acre field, stretching so far as to be weirdly lonely at the very far end. Every part of it was distinct. You turned to the left as you entered by a heavy hedge of wild-rose and blackberry. There the wild convolvulus blew its white trumpet gloriously and violets ran over the bank under the green veil, and stellaria and speedwell made in May a mimic heaven. I remember a meadow there, and yet again a potato-digging, where we picked our own potatoes for dinner and grew sun-burnt as the brown men and women who required so many cans of well-water to drink at their work. Where the hedge curved there was a little passage, through which the dyke-water flowed into the next field. It was delightful to set little boats of leaf and grass upon the stream, and to see them carried gaily by the current down that arcade of green light. Some of the inquisitive ones waded after them, and emerged wet and muddy in the next field. I preferred to keep the mystery of the place, and to believe it went a long, long way. For half the length of the field the water flowed over long grass that lay face downward in it. To see it you had to lift the grass and the meadow flowers. Once we were startled there in a summer dusk before the hay was cut, when all the corncrakes were crying out that summer was in the land. As we threaded the meadow aisles, a heavy, dark body leapt from its lair and into the dyke. It was a badger, we learnt afterwards, and its presence there gave the place an attractive fearsomeness. Half-way down, where a boundary hedge had once made two fields of the Ten Acres, the low hedge changed to a tall wall of stately thorn trees. Below their feet the stream ran, amber, pellucid, over a line of transformed pebbles. By this we used to lie for hours, watching the silver-scaled minnows as they sailed on. At the far end there was watercress, and over the hedge a strange field, good for mushrooms, but which bore with us a somewhat uncanny reputation.

Across it you saw the gray house-chimneys of the lonely house reputed to be haunted. Opposite its door stood an old fort on a little hill, a noted resort of the fairies. Any summer gloaming at all, you might see their hundreds of little lamps threading a fantastic measure in and out on the rath. I never heard that any one saw more of them than those lights, which floated away if any were bold enough to approach them, like glorified balls of that thistledown of which children divine what's o'clock.

At the other side of the Ten Acres was a fantastic corner of grass, which was always a miniature meadow. There swung the scarlet and black butterflies which have flown into Fairyland,

and there the corncrake built her nest in the grass. It was a famous corner for bird's-nesting, which with us took no crueller form than liking to part the thick leaves to peep at the pretty, perturbed mother-thrush on her clutch. Sometimes we peeped too often, and she flew away and left the eggs cold. We saw the world from that corner, for one could see through the hedge on to the road by lying low where the roots of the hedge-row made a thinness. We should not have cared about this if it were not that we could look, unseen ourselves, at the infrequent passer-by, for the hedge grew luxuriantly. Further down it became partly a clay bank, and there on the coarse grass used to hang snail-shells of all sizes, and, as I remember them, of shining gold and silver. The inhabitant was the drawback to all that beauty, yet when we found an empty house, it was cold, dull, and with the sheen vanished.

Across the road was the moat-field, the great fascination of which was in the wild hill that gave it its name. What the moat originally was I know not. I think, now, it must have been a gravel-hill, for it was full of deep gashes, of pits and quarries, run over by briar, alight with furze-bushes. It must have been long disused, for the hedge that was set around it—to keep the cattle out, perhaps—was tall and sturdy, and grew up boldly towards the trees that studded it at intervals. There was no other entry to it except by gaps we made in the close hedge, and, wriggling through these, we climbed among briars and all kinds of vegetation that made a miniature jungle overhead. Near the top we emerged on stunted grass, with the wide sky over us, and before us the champaign country stretching to the plains of Meath, and the smoke of the city, and the misty sea. Southwards there were the eternal hills which grow so dear to one, yet never so intimate that they have not fresh exquisite surprises in store. We threaded the moat by paths between the furze, on the golden honey-hives of which fluttered moths like blue turquoise. The dragon-fly was there, and the lady-bird and little beetles in emerald coats of mail. And over that the lark soared in a wide field of air to hail God at His own very gates. Bitter little sloes grew on the moat, and blackberries in their season; and if you had descended into one of the many cups of the place, even long before the sun had begun to slant, you liked to shout to your companions and be answered cheerily from the human world. The moat had an uncanniness of its own; it was haunted by leaping fires that overran it and left no trace. You might see it afar, suffused by a dull glare, any dim summer night. So have I myself beheld it when I have crept through the dews on a nocturnal expedition: and though one of the commonplace suggested that it might have been the new moon rising scarlet behind the luxuriant vegetation of the moat, that was in the unimaginative next day, and not when we discussed the marvel in the scented darkness that comes between summer eve and dawn.

Then there was the well-field, where a little stream that fed the well clattered over pebbles, made leaps so sudden down tiny inclines that we called the commotion a waterfall, and widened under a willow-tree into a pool, brown and still, where, tradition said, had once been seen a trout. For sake of this glorious memory we fished long with squirming worms and a pin, but caught not even the silliest little minnow. This small game we used to bag, by the way, at will, by simply lowering a can into the green depths of the well, where there was always a tiny silver fin a-sailing. Once we kept a pair three days in the water-jug, and finally restored them to their emerald dark. The well-field was in part marshy and ended in a rushy place, where water-cresses grew thick, and a little bridge led into the neighbour's fields. There we found yellow iris, and the purple bee orchis, and fox-gloves.

Hard by was Nano's Field, which we affected only in the autumn, for then we gathered crab-apples, of a yellow and pink, most delightful to the eye. And also the particular variety of blackberry which ripens first, and is large and of irregular shape, but, to the common blackberry, what purple grapes are to the thin, green variety. And again, there was the front lawn, where the quicken-berry hung in drooping scarlet clusters above us, as we sat on a knoll, and a sea of gold and white washed about us in May. But the fields make me garrulous, and if I were to go on they that never tired the children might weary the grown listener. Said I not they were seldom visited? Yet their enchantment is still there for happy generations unborn. The children and the fields and the birds we have always with us. I would that for every child there might be the fields, to make long after a dream of green beauty, though the world has grown arid. Because the dream seems so sweet to me I have gossiped of it, but have not named half its delicate delights, nor some of the great ones: as the romps in the hay fields, the voyage of discovery after hens' nests, the mysteries of that double hedge that is the orchard boundary, and the hidden places in gnarled boughs, where you perched among the secrets of the birds and the leaves, and saw the crescent moon through a tender veil of enchantment while yet the orange of the sunset was in the west.

Sweet Singer from Over the Sea

A Chat with Katharine Tynan

As I walked up from the station (writes a representative of *The Sketch*), and made my way through the rows of prim villas to the still countrified cottage, standing on the edge of breezy country, to which Miss Katharine Tynan (now Mrs. Harry Hinkson) has removed her household gods, I could not help thinking of her early home, beautiful White Hall, Clondalkin, at the foot of the Dublin Mountains, where it had once been my privilege and pleasure to see her, and which she has herself so exquisitely described in her last volume of verse—

> A low horizon hems me in,
> Low hills with fields of gold between,
> Woods that are waving, veiled with grey,
> A little river far away,
> Birds on the boughs, and on the sward
> Daisies that, dancing, praise the Lord.
>
> Outside my window I can see
> The bent boughs of an apple-tree,
> Where little fruits turn rosier;
> And every evening of the year
> I watch the golden sunsets die
> Yonder in the wide Western sky.

But soon the apparent limits of the London suburb are passed, and it becomes easy to see why Ealing has proved dear to more than one poetic heart, for among Mrs. Hinkson's nearest neighbours is Mr. Austin Dobson.

A little gate swings back, and you are welcomed with true Irish hospitality, not only by the lady you have come to see, but by Paddy, a huge St. Bernard, who seems to have taken quite kindly to an alien soil. Mrs. Hinkson's bright little study-parlour has already assumed a homelike and characteristic air. Fine photographs of Dante Gabriel Rossetti's pictures, given to the young Irish poetess by the dead painter's brother, Mr. William Rossetti, hang in close proximity to her writing-table, and give even a stranger an insight into her complex personality. Close to the beautiful and severe "Girlhood of Mary" hangs "Proserpine", and "Mary Magdalene and the door of Simon, the Pharisee", "Dante's Dream", the portrait of Christina Rossetti and her mother, and a striking counterfeit presentment of the artist himself, show how true and wide are Mrs. Hinkson's sympathies.

In a few picturesque words she describes her happy childhood in the Dominican convent. "No, I do not think I was at all a literary child," she says, smiling; and then is brought out for your inspection a quaint prayer-book, in which the "Katie" of fifteen years ago jotted down her thoughts in church, when the service seemed to her too long or uninteresting—sentences written in a bold, childish hand, which show that there was not a little of the "old Adam" left, notwithstanding all the good nuns could do.

"I began writing," she continues, "when I was about seventeen, and my first volume, *Louise de la Vallière and Other Poems*, was published in 1885. It went into two editions, and made me many unknown friends, among others, the late Lord Lytton, Aubrey de Vere, Sir Samuel Ferguson, Cardinal Newman, and Alice Meynell—all wrote me the kindest letters, and when I came to London shortly after, I made the acquaintance of the Rossettis and of many others whom I had never expected to know save through their books."

"You must possess many curious autographs," I venture to observe.

"I will show you what I have," she answers simply, and produces a quaint black book, in which are placed some two score of precious letters, including a long epistle from Cardinal Manning, in which he pays his correspondent the high compliment of saying, "The least merit in your poems is the very pure diction." No small tribute from a man who, not to please his best friend, would have condescended to the least flattery.

"I believe that you have written not a little prose, as well as poetry, Mrs. Hinkson?"

"Many years passed before I attempted to write in prose. First I brought out a second volume of verse entitled *Shamrocks*, then an American editor, who knew my work, asked me to try writing some articles for him, and since then I have written constantly for both American and English magazines and reviews. But the only prose book which I have published was the Life of Mother Xaviera Fallon, the Superioress-General of the Loretto Order. I called it *A Nun, Her Friends, and Her Order*, and, of course, it was greatly compiled from notes given me by the sisters who had known her. Last year I edited a selection of Irish love-songs for Mr. Fisher Unwin, and brought out my third volume of poetry, *Ballads and Lyrics*. But Messrs. Mathews and Lane will publish some time this autumn more of my verse, and I hope soon to bring out a collection of short stories, or rather sketches, of Irish life."

"Then have you any regular time for work, or do you allow inspiration to be your taskmaster?"

"I find that I can do my best writing in the evening, but I have no fixed rule, and work as I feel able."

And then, as we walk up and down the path which winds through the green, sweet-smelling wilderness, fast turning into a charming cottage garden, where fruit, flowers, and the elements of a kitchen garden struggle together for mastery, Mrs. Hinkson tells me a little of the ardent interest she takes in Irish politics, past and present.

"You will understand something of our views," she says softly, "when I tell you that there is a portrait of Mr. Parnell in every room in our house"; and then, in answer to a discreet question, she confides the fact that, although he claims no pretensions to being a brother-poet, her husband has strong literary sympathies and tastes, and wrote on the occasion of Trinity College's Tercentenary an account of "Student Life in Trinity College", of which ancient *alma mater* he was alternately both student and tutor. Even at the present time, though actively engaged in other work, Mr. Hinkson has found time to translate a novel from the German.

"And do you like London," I ask as a last question, "after lovely Clondalkin?"

"Comparisons are odious," she replies contentedly. "I do not think I should care to live altogether in town; but next winter I hope to see a little more of the world. For the present I have only found time to attend one or two literary dinners."

Ghost Story of a Novelist

Mrs. Katharine Tynan relates a Weird Tale
—May Be a Coincidence.

Mrs. Katharine Tynan, the well-known novelist, sends to the *Daily Graphic* the following weird story:

"This may be a coincidence. On the other hand, it may be a ghost story. It happened to one near and dear to me. It was in his college days, and it was a long vacation, during which he had elected to stay on in his college rooms and work. The rooms were at the top of one of the highest houses in the ancient foundation of Queen Elizabeth, T.C.D. [Trinity College Dublin]. There was not a soul in the house but himself, and the quads and buildings were full of echoing emptiness after nightfall. He was not nervous in the ordinary sense of the word, and did not object to his solitude in his eyrie, although an impressionable Celtic visitor calling on him one afternoon remarked that he would not occupy those rooms in the empty house in the empty college for a single night, no matter what inducement were offered to him to do it.

"It was a night or two later. The sole occupant of No. — awoke in the dark. He had been awakened by an unusual sound on the stairs. He heard the foot ascend and pause outside his door. He sprang out of bed, and fumbled for a light. By the time he had got it, he heard the foot going downstairs again. He hurried to his door, opened it and listened. All was silent as the grave in the empty house. He returned to bed mystified, and slept till morning. In the morning, as he made his own breakfast, and thought of his mysterious visitor of the night before, he glanced toward the door, and noticed something white half-way under the door—a visiting card. He picked it up. It was the card of a man he knew—a college acquaintance, whom we shall call Roland White. In the corner of the card was written in pencil, 'Just passing through.' The mystery was not cleared. Why on earth should Roland White have called in the dead waste and middle of the night? He had heard of him a few days before as enjoying himself thoroughly grouse-shooting in the west.

"A day or two passed. As he came into college one afternoon he was stopped by one of the porters. 'Very sad about poor Mr. White, sir?' 'What about Mr. White?' 'Haven't you heard, sir? It's in the evening papers.' It was the familiar accident of the trigger of a gun catching in a twig as the sportsman scrambled through a fence. Shot in the head, Roland White had died within a few minutes of the accident. The coincidence would have been if the card was an old one, and had been dislodged from somewhere or another to lie below the door on the very night following the day when the fatal accident had occurred. But then the foot on the stairs in the middle of the night! Ghost story or coincidence, it remains a mystery to this day."

Dunsany

On a day when we were sitting in the library at Shankill A.E. told us, among other things, about a picture of Lord Dunsany's of a great snowy waste, with the print of footsteps going across it, just the footsteps. I was rather fascinated by the idea—very Dunsanyesque—and I wrote some verses to accompany the picture, and sent them to Lord Dunsany. A little later I had this letter.

s.s. Adolf Woermann,
Off Port Said, Dec. 29th.

Dear Mrs. Hinkson,—Of course I remember meeting you: one does not meet a poet every day. I remember that you told me you had just read a tale of mine in the *Celtic Christmas*, and I was glad you liked it. I've been away lion-hunting, but I'll send you the picture as soon as I get home, which should be in a few days after you get this. I'd be delighted if it's any use to you, but I'm afraid the presence of a somewhat gruesome beast that is nosing along after the footsteps may spoil it for you. I think the poem is charming.

The picture is very roughly something like this:
(He drew a very weird pen-and-ink sketch. A bit of snowy land bounded by mountain peaks. All around space and the stars. The footsteps, and the beast following, and at the edge of Space is written, "The End.")

It all happened on a very thin world. You can see the stars above it and stars underneath. The beast was supposed to be Remorse, following some one all his life. But this sketch is rather a mess. I'll send you the other soon. I'm afraid it will be no good to you. It was a great pleasure to see your poem.

I don't know what became of that poem. Probably I shall find it some day in a book.

A little later we, my Pamela and I, went down to the Dunsanys. With Lady Dunsany one fell in love at once. Nothing could be sweeter, gentler, more charming. Lord Dunsany was, I soon found, of the intemperate talkers, of which I was very glad, because he paralysed me with shyness. He was well worth listening to. He is a big, boyish man, who gives one the impression of always having had his own way; but though he seemed overbearing in argument at first, and reduced my opposition, such as it was, to pulp, he was really very simple and in a sense gentle. He was like Stevenson's Henley, who would roar you down in an argument and finally, after a deal of sound and fury, would discover that you had points of agreement all the time.

Dunsany kept a glorious tea-table in those pre-war days. That first time I was too shy of Lord Dunsany to enjoy my tea, but I watched him enjoying his, surrounded by battalions of little glass pots containing all sorts of jams and honey, quite delicious to look at, to say nothing of lavish supplies of cream, hot cakes, all manner of sandwiches and tea-table delicacies. I am sure I could have made a tremendous tea, but I did not: instead I ate delicately and listened to Lord Dunsany demolishing the work of the Christian era, especially in Rome, where he said Christianity had destroyed the magnificent Pagan Art. At last I said in a small and trembling voice: "Will no one say a word for Christianity?" But no one did, though Lady Dunsany said, laughing, that Dunsany was saying more than he meant, and that Christianity had plenty to be said for it.

That evening I was rejoiced when Lord Dunsany brought out his pictures to show me—extraordinary pictures, as strange and fascinating as his stories. Afterwards he read the stories, rolling out the magnificent names and the sonorous procession of the words with great enjoyment to himself and me. Usually I become sleepy while being read to, but I did not feel at all sleepy. I knew he was enjoying himself, as I was, and what could a good guest or a good host wish for more?

It was very amusing to hear Lord Dunsany talk about his experience with publishers, who, being business men, took it for granted that Lord Dunsany—a rich man and a genius—would be content with glory and leave the filthy lucre to them. They were distressed when the noble author insisted on the business side of the agreement. A little later Sidney Sime was telling at Dunsany how much joy it gave Lord Howard de Walden to receive a cheque for two guineas, earned by his pen. After all it must be a delight to those to whom money comes without any effort of their own to *earn* it. It explains why Society ladies contribute to the magazines, and the strenuous young aristocrat occasionally goes off to work with his hands.

I remember an amusing thing Lord Dunsany told us, in a certain vein of indignation, of an application received from a London illustrated paper, offering him two or three guineas if he would contribute to a symposium "What it Feels Like to be a Millionaire". He replied that they had better ask Lord Howard de Walden since he did not happen to be a millionaire and could not know what a millionaire felt like. He received an effusive letter of thanks for his interest in the symposium, saying in conclusion that the Editor had acted upon his kind advice and written to Lord Howard de

Walden, asking him to state for the benefit of their readers what it felt like to be a millionaire.

Like all geniuses Lord Dunsany is very simple. At dinner that first evening he asked me if I used salt or bone-dust, and went on to explain that some one he had met in a railway carriage had told him that a certain table condiment had a large proportion of bone dust in its composition. He grew very excited over the matter, imagining what bones. It was almost as lurid as the Times *Kadaververwertungsanstalt*. After that occasion every time I met him at table I asked him carelessly if he used salt or bone dust. He always rose eagerly. "Oh, you know about that, do you? It's extraordinary how few people know! You are the first person I've met, in fact . . . "

It was a charming house to stay at. Lady Dunsany would have made any house charming, and Lord Dunsany was, of course, extraordinarily interesting and very kind, with the simplicity which was lovable and provocative.

(I am afraid I speak of him as though he, as well as those happy visits, were in the past tense, which, very happily for many things and people, he is not.)

The hall at Dunsany was full of the heads of his big-game shooting—terrible heads. Sidney Sime, that cynical person, whom we met there—he was already an old friend of my husband—in the early summer of the fateful year, professed to regard them as no more than common trophies of slaughter—like legs of mutton, for example. This point of view puzzled and somewhat depressed Lord Dunsany.

He talked literature to me usually, but one day he discussed rabbit stalking as a substitute for big-game stalking, and waxed enthusiastic about it.

"Oh, by Jove!" he said, "it is grand sport. They have such fine ears and they are off like the wind." One had a mental picture of bison or antelope, but it was really rabbits. "If the sun is behind you it throws your shadow; then it is difficult and exciting, you have to hide behind every grass blade as you get nearer and nearer . . . "

Lord Dunsany is six-foot-four of height.

The atmosphere of the house was very literary. Lady Dunsany had grown up to literature. Her father and mother, when Lord Jersey was Governor of Australia, made a pilgrimage to Samoa to see Robert Louis Stevenson. I have said that A.E. said of Lady Lytton that she was more like a flower than any woman he ever saw. Lady Dunsany was—is—very flower-like, a pansy perhaps, or a wild anemone, something delicate and shy, kind and gentle. I think all the talk was about literary people and things. To be literary was to have the entrée to Dunsany; I don't think other people counted.

The day after our arrival Lord Dunsany went out hunting, and we motored with Lady Dunsany to the meet of the Meath Hounds, taking Tara on our way. It was a very wild day, and when I was asked afterwards my impressions of Tara I said it was a Big Wind, which pleased Lady Dunsany: I have heard of that saying of mine from an English correspondent whom I have never seen, since then.

Padraic Colum had been at Dunsany just before us, and had told little Randal Plunkett, the only son, of various charms which would enable him to see the palace on Tara and the Kings and Queens and Knights and Ladies. I might have seen them, in the wind perhaps, if I had not been trying to keep on my hat.

Lord Dunsany talked a good deal of Francis Ledwidge, of whose discovery he was very proud, calling him always "Mr. Ledwidge".

When we went there again in the early summer we found H.G. and Mrs. Wells already there. They came in from the river to the glorious tea. I had always been very much alarmed of H.G. Wells, because of a sentence in one of his books. What that sentence was and why it should have alarmed me is known only to myself. Very much to my stupefaction I found myself walking up and down, up and down, with him in the avenue outside after tea. I was quite pleased with myself for being so little afraid; but the next morning when I was walking with him again the terror returned. I was dumb. I thought he was inordinately bored; perhaps he was; we could see Lady Dunsany sitting under a tree in the distance teaching Randal his lessons. I asked myself why any one should want to talk to me with that distant prospect of Lady Dunsany.

"Don't you feel that you want to go and do some work?" I said to him. "I am often taken that way myself, being accustomed to industrious mornings."

He said he did feel like that and went away, but he came back in a very short time and joined Lady Dunsany and me under the tree, accusing me of having rudely driven him away because I wanted to talk to Lady Dunsany. But it wasn't that, though Lady Dunsany was very good to talk to.

I admired Mr. Wells's *sang-froid* next morning, when, while we waited for Lady Dunsany's appearance at the breakfast-table, the big spirit-lamp under the kettle went a-fire. He was sitting half-in, half-out the open window, explaining that it was an excellent position from which to run away if the fire spread. It did spread, to the tablecloth. I rang the bell frantically: no one else did anything. Presently the butler came in and, without flurry, enveloped the conflagration in a large table napkin, putting it out. We must have looked fools to him. One realised then the superiority of the trained man to the mere intellectual.

Some of the party spent the morning on the river in canoes. It was a small and muddy river. I preferred *terra firma*, especially as Randal had danced about us, shrieking joyfully: "O Mummie, they've got the leaky boat. Isn't it fun?" It was Mr. Wells and Pam who had the leaky boat. But the morning passed without mishap. Lord Dunsany had gone off cricketing, Sidney Sime and Joseph Holbrook arrived for lunch. Sidney Sime was another person I was secretly afraid of. He had declined to illustrate a poem of mine, which my husband had sent to him, with somewhat mordant comments. And there was something merciless about his brilliant drawings as I remembered them: I might have said "heartless and soulless" before I met him. We talked of mysticism—of all things!—on the tennis-lawn after lunch. I am glad to believe that he was sincerely sorry when he learnt that we were leaving that afternoon. He and Joseph Holbrook came to see us later at Shankill. The latter had already set a lyric of mine "Summer-Sweet" to music, so we were, in a sense, old friends. When the war is over I hope to finish that talk with Sidney Sime.

After all we were fortunate in our meeting with H.G. Wells. My thirteen-year-old Pam had just finished *Mr. Polly*. She had all the gags of it by heart. He could not but be pleased: these are the kind of things which please an author. He made a sketch in her autograph-book of Mr. Polly, sitting on the stile, murmuring "Rotten, beastly stinkin' 'ole!" after Mrs. Polly had given him that nice meal of cold pork and pickled onions and cheese. Pam also instructed him on the Irish question, a fact to which he has referred in *Mr. Britling Sees It Through*.

One of those days Lord Dunsany talked to Pam about his big-game-hunting in something of these terms:

"While we breakfasted I said carelessly: 'Well, what are we going to do to-day?' 'Oh,' said my hunter, 'I have my own little game on to-day. I will tell you later.' So, afterwards, when we had mounted our horses he disclosed his plan to me. We were just inside the border of the lion country, and he told me that about 4 o'clock that morning two lions had come down to the river beside which we camped, to drink, and had roared lustily for about five minutes, through which I had slept soundly: so he proposed hunting for the day's work. I agreed, and we set off; but luck seemed to have deserted us that day. All the morning we hunted, but it was midday before we sighted game, and it was not a lion.

"I was going a little ahead of my hunter when I perceived an enormous rhinoceros standing about thirty yards away, and beyond him another, and beyond that one yet another, and another. It so happened that my hunter did not see the three beyond the first one, but only the leader; however, I did not know this at the time. When he said 'Shoot', pointing at the leader, I raised my gun and fired. The rhinoceros swung round and dashed blindly past us, the herd clattering behind. I fired again and missed: I fired again and again, only wounding him, until, just as he was charging, and it was death for either of us, I fired and killed him. The herd, furious when they saw him fall, charged in a body, but they went past us, and stopped with their heads up, sniffing the air. Then they wheeled about and galloped off into the forest.

"We dragged the dead rhinoceros down to the river, and that night we camped near him. When darkness fell we went out and sat near him, with our loaded rifles across our knees, waiting for the lions which we knew would come to devour the remains. The frogs all started barking with the coming of night, and kept up a regular concert, barking against each other. And then, quite suddenly, every sound ceased. There was not a movement on the water nor on the land except the stealthy pad-pad of the lions.

"Sitting there in the darkness one realised how trivial all the things of the civilised world were beside this great thing, and how far away seemed that other world of peaceful towns and villages and farms from this wilderness where we sat clutching our rifles and waiting for the king of beasts.

"Then a most extraordinary thing happened. We were suddenly enveloped in a thick mist, which wrapped us round

Dunsany

as in a cloak so that we could see nothing, but we knew by the growling and roaring of the lions that they had found their meat. All that night we sat there, while the lions roared close beside us; but, just before dawn, they became quiet, and when the mist cleared there was nothing to be seen but a single hyaena who stood out for a moment from the forest, and fled at the sight of two men sitting with rifles across their knees."

I have not seen Lord Dunsany since that June of 1914. Lady Dunsany came to lunch at Shankill a little later to meet the two poets, Joseph and Nancy Campbell. Nancy Campbell she knew already as Nancy Maude, who had made a very romantic marriage.

We were to have gone to Dunsany very soon afterwards, but all those plans went down before the events of August 1914. Black Monday had come and gone when Pamela and my husband met Lord Dunsany in that wonderful room at the top of Plunkett House, where the *Irish Homestead* is edited under the eyes of Angels and Archangels, Powers, Principalities, Dominions. Sidney Sime said, visiting that room: "So this is where turnips are made! Good Lord, it's a mad world!" Lord Dunsany was saying: "I shall never come back. None of the officers will come back, certainly not a man of my height." And again he was denouncing the local politicians, with characteristic whirlwind energy, and listening with a certain unexpected sweet reasonableness to my husband's defence of them.

I asked Lady Dunsany once if she was not alarmed when he was absent on his lion-hunting expeditions, with no news coming through from him. She said, "I know he is a very good shot."

Here in the West of Ireland where literature is held in little honour, except by an occasional priest, I sigh for such a house as Dunsany. How different life would be if our lot had placed us in Meath rather than in Mayo!

Sources

"The First Wife" was collected in *An Isle in the Water*. London: Adam & Charles Black, 1895.

"The Dead Mother" was collected in *Shamrocks*. London: K. Paul, Trench, 1887.

"The Sea's Dead" was collected in *An Isle in the Water*. London: Adam & Charles Black, 1895.

"The Dead Tryst" appeared in *Atalanta* (December 1892).

"The Death Spancel" was first published in *The Speaker* (17 August 1895); it was collected in *An Isle in the Water*. London: Adam & Charles Black, 1895.

"The Death-Watch" was appeared in *The Scots Observer* (14 December 1889); it was collected in *Ballads and Lyrics*. London: K. Paul, Trench, Trübner, 1891.

"The Ghosts" is an extract from *The Story of Bawn*. London: Smith, Elder, 1906.

"A Bride from the Dead" was first published in *The Weekly Tale-Teller* (22 October 1910).

"Miss Mary" was first published in *The Sketch* (1 July 1903).

"The Ghost" was collected in *Innocencies: A Book of Verse*. London: A. H. Bullen, 1905.

"A Sentence of Death" was first published in *The Story-Teller* (May 1908); it was reprinted in *The Ash-Tree Press Annual Macabre 2005*, edited by Jack Adrian. Ashcroft: Ash-Tree Press, 2005.

"The Dead Coach" was first published in *The National Observer* (2 July 1892); it was collected in *Cuckoo Songs*. London: Elkin Matthews and John Lane, 1884. It was reprinted in *The Haunted Hour*, compiled by Margaret Widdemar. New York: Harcourt, Brace & Howe, 1920.

"The Body Snatching" was first published in *The Sketch* (15 January 1902); it also appeared in *The Province* (Vancouver), 14 February 1902.

"The Ghost" was first published in *Black and White* (22 March 1902).

"The Spancel of Death" was first published in the *Weekly Freeman Summer Sketch Book* (July 1890); it also appeared, uncredited, in *Arbroath Herald and Advertiser for the Montrose Burghs* (14/28 November 1901). An apology for copyright infringement issued on 1 May 1902.

"The Dream House" was first published in *The Story-Teller* (January 1909); it was reprinted in *The Ash-Tree Press Annual Macabre 2005*, edited by Jack Adrian. Ashcroft: Ash-Tree Press, 2005.

"The Call" was collected in *Innocencies: A Book of Verse*. London: A. H. Bullen, 1905.

Sources

"A Night in the Cathedral" was first published in *The Weekly Tale-Teller* (9 April 1910).

"The Little Ghost" [Story] was first published in *The Grand Magazine* (June 1913); it was collected in *Lovers' Meeting*. London: T. Werner Laurie, 1914.

"The Little Ghost" [Poem] was first published in *The Spectator* (14 January 1911); it was collected in *New Poems*. London: Sidgwick & Jackson, 1911. It was reprinted in *The Haunted Hour*, compiled by Margaret Widdemar. New York: Harcourt, Brace & Howe, 1920.

"The Picture on the Wall" was first published in *English Illustrated Magazine* (December 1895); it was reprinted in *Victorian Ghost Stories*, edited by Montague Summers. London: Fortune Press, 1933.

"The Fields of My Childhood" was collected in *An Isle in the Water*. London: Adam & Charles Black, 1895.

☙

"Sweet Singer from Over the Sea: A Chat with Katharine Tynan" was first published in *The Sketch* (13 September 1893); it was reprinted in *The Green Book 14*, Autumn 2019.

"Ghost Story of a Novelist" appeared in *The Winnipeg Tribune* (10 October 1905); it was reprinted in *The Green Book 14*, Autumn 2019.

"Dunsany" is an extract from *The Years of the Shadow*. London: Constable & Co., 1919; it was reprinted in *The Green Book 10*, Autumn 2017.

Acknowledgements

Dedicated to the memory of Richard Dalby, whose unwavering scholarship, as well as his "Mistresses of the Macabre" series for Sarob Press, paved the way for this collection.

The publisher would like to thank to Mike Ashley, Peter Bell, Nathalie Boisard Beudin, Rob Brown, Brian Coldrick, Timothy J. Jarvis, Meggan Kehrli, Ken Mackenzie, Jim Rockhill, and the late Richard Dalby for their assistance in the compilation and production of this volume, the first to showcase the supernatural and macabre works of Katharine Tynan. Many of these stories are collected and reprinted here for the first time.

About the Author

Katharine Tynan (1859-1931) was born in Dublin and raised at Whitehall, the family home in Clondalkin. Her literary salon there attracted notables such as W. B. Yeats, with whom she formed a lifelong friendship. Tynan became a prolific writer, authoring more than a hundred novels in addition to memoirs and numerous volumes of poetry. Her works deal with feminism, Catholicism, and nationalism—Yeats declared of her early collection *Shamrocks* (1887) that "in finding her nationality, she has also found herself".

SWAN RIVER PRESS

Founded in 2003, Swan River Press is an independent publishing company, based in Dublin, Ireland, dedicated to gothic, supernatural, and fantastic literature. We specialise in limited edition hardbacks, publishing fiction from around the world with an emphasis on Ireland's contributions to the genre.

www.swanriverpress.ie

*"Handsome, beautifully made volumes . . .
altogether irresistible."*

– Michael Dirda, *Washington Post*

*"It [is] often down to small, independent, specialist presses
to keep the candle of horror fiction flickering . . . "*

– Darryl Jones, *Irish Times*

*"Swan River Press has emerged as one of the most inspiring
new presses over the past decade. Not only are the books
beautifully presented and professionally produced, but they
aspire consistently to high literary quality and originality,
ranging from current writers of supernatural/weird fiction
to rare or forgotten works by departed authors."*

– Peter Bell, *Ghosts & Scholars*

BENDING TO EARTH
Strange Stories by Irish Women

edited by Maria Giakaniki
and Brian J. Showers

Irish women have long produced literature of the gothic, uncanny, and supernatural. *Bending to Earth* draws together twelve such tales. While none of the authors herein were considered primarily writers of fantastical fiction during their lifetimes, they each wandered at some point in their careers into more speculative realms—some only briefly, others for lengthier stays.

Names such as Charlotte Riddell and Rosa Mulholland will already be familiar to aficionados of the eerie, while Katharine Tynan and Clotilde Graves are sure to gain new admirers. From a ghost story in the Swiss Alps to a premonition of death in the West of Ireland to strange rites in a South Pacific jungle, *Bending to Earth* showcases a diverse range of imaginative writing which spans the better part of a century.

"Bending to Earth *is full of tales of women walled-up in rooms, of vengeful or unforgetting dead wives, of mistreated lovers, of cruel and murderous husbands.*"

– Darryl Jones, *Irish Times*

"*A surprising, extraordinary anthology featuring twelve uncanny and supernatural stories from the nineteenth century . . . highly recommended, extremely enjoyable.*"

– *British Fantasy Society*

NOT TO BE TAKEN AT BED-TIME
and Other Strange Stories

Rosa Mulholland

In the late-nineteenth century Rosa Mulholland (1841-1921) achieved great popularity and acclaim for her many novels, written for both an adult audience and younger readers. Several of these novels chronicled the lives of the poor, often incorporating rural Irish settings and folklore. Earlier in her career, Mulholland became one of the select band of authors employed by Charles Dickens to write stories for his popular magazine *All the Year Round*, together with Wilkie Collins, Elizabeth Gaskell, Joseph Sheridan Le Fanu, and Amelia B. Edwards.

Mulholland's best supernatural and weird short stories have been gathered together in the present collection, edited and introduced by Richard Dalby, to celebrate this gifted late Victorian "Mistress of the Macabre".

"It's a mark of a good writer that they can be immersed in the literary culture of their time and yet manage to transcend it, and Mulholland does that with the tales collected here."

– David Longhorn, *Supernatural Tales*

"NUMBER NINETY"
& Other Ghost Stories

B. M. Croker

The bestselling Irish author B. M. Croker enjoyed a highly successful literary career from 1880 until her death forty years later. Her novels were witty and fast moving, set mostly in India and her native Ireland. Titles such as *Proper Pride* (1882) and *Diana Barrington* (1888) found popularity for their mix of romantic drama and Anglo-Indian military life. And, like many late-Victorian authors, Croker also wrote ghost stories for magazines and Christmas annuals. From the colonial nightmares such as "The Dâk Bungalow at Dakor" and "The North Verandah" to the more familiar streets of haunted London in "Number Ninety", this collection showcases fifteen of B. M. Croker's most effective supernatural tales.

"This is a solid collection of stories that deserve to be better known . . . they are all enjoyable ghostly tales, and ideal reading for the long winter nights."

– Supernatural Tales

"[Croker's] Indian stories evoke colonial life vividly . . . What makes them all readable are the well-observed characters and settings"

– Wormwood

EARTH-BOUND
and Other Supernatural Tales

Dorothy Macardle

Originally published in 1924, the nine tales that comprise Earth-Bound were written by Dorothy Macardle while she was held a political prisoner in Dublin's Kilmainham Gaol and Mountjoy Prison. The stories incorporate themes that intrigued her throughout her life; themes out of the myths and legends of Ireland; ghostly interventions, dreams and premonitions, clairvoyance, and the Otherworld in parallel with this one. It is so easy to dismiss them, as some have, merely as part of the narrative of "Irish nationalism" of the time, but it is the supernatural elements that make them much more. She would revisit these themes in later works such as her classic haunted house novel *The Uninvited* (1941). To this new edition of Macardle's debut collection, reprinted for the first time in ninety years, we have added four more tales of the supernatural.

"Beautifully written, with a fine air for the music of language and vivid descriptions of the landscape."

– Black Static

"A beautifully presented and valuable resource for anyone interested in Irish history, culture or literature."

– Dublin Inquirer

THE GREEN BOOK
*Writings on Irish Gothic,
Supernatural and Fantastic Literature*

edited by
Brian J. Showers

Aimed at a general readership and published twice-yearly, *The Green Book* features commentaries, articles, and reviews on Irish Gothic, Supernatural and Fantastic literature.

Certainly favourites such as Bram Stoker and John Connolly will come to mind, but *The Green Book* also showcases Ireland's other notable fantasists: Fitz-James O'Brien, Charlotte Riddell, Lafcadio Hearn, Rosa Mulholland, J. Sheridan Le Fanu, Cheiro, Harry Clarke, Dorothy Macardle, Lord Dunsany, Elizabeth Bowen, C. S. Lewis, Mervyn Wall, Conor McPherson . . . and many others.

*"A welcome addition to the realm of accessible
nonfiction about supernatural horror."*

– Ellen Datlow

*"Eminently readable . . . [an] engaging little journal
that treads the path between accessibility and
academic depth with real panache."*

– Peter Tenant, *Black Static*

CPSIA information can be obtained
at www.ICGtesting.com
Printed in the USA
BVHW071154231222
654913BV00022B/279